The Shop Girl
of
Flowergate

ELLEN L. EKSTROM

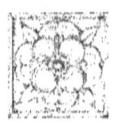

WHYTE ROSE & VIOLET, SCRIBES

Whyte Rose & Violet, Scribes Publishing Edition

Copyright 2017, Ellen L. Ekstrom

Second Edition, Copyright 2021

The Shop Girl of Flowergate

ISBN-13: 978-0692474785

Published in the United States of America

Cover design: Whyte Rose & Violet Artists
Images courtesy Robyn of Exeter via Adobe Stock
and Susan Stewart, iStockPhoto.com

WHYTE ROSE & VIOLET, SCRIBES
Berkeley, California
www.whyteroseandviolet.net

To my guardian angel, JS.

The Shop Girl
of
Flowergate

Chapter 1

THE ONLY WINDOW in my bed-chamber looks out over the sea. For a long while, I had to stand on a stack of books or shove a chest across the room to reach the sill because while the casement is long and tall, I am not. I was fortunate that Master Foyle, the carpenter in Sullen, made a special contraption with steps like a ladder and a large platform. I call it my throne.

One day I shall have my real throne back.

But that is another day, and now I have this convenient contraption. It's made climbing easier and my pastime of looking out more enjoyable. I often take my needlework there, be it knitting or making lace; sometimes, I bring a book. The smell of the sea, the sound of the waves, and the touch of the wind on my face, the warmth of the sun when it deigns to shine, remind me that there is something more in the world than this small castle with its large tower, this place by the sea at the most northern point of my father's kingdom.

I've stopped counting how many days I've been here.

They said it was for my safety, being taken here to be away from The War. No one would want to come this far north to take a princess for ransom. Once you passed the Sapphire Hills, the wind and rain lashed at the moors and forests, and it sometimes lasted for weeks. There were no great lords manors, for it was a forsaken place and at the edge of nowhere, which led to the Great Sea. If you had affection for sheep, I suppose you'd grow to love Flowergate.

Flowergate. A clever name, that.

We saw flowers perhaps one month out of the year, but they were unlike any in the south once they bloomed. The colors could blind you with their radiance, and it was said their scents were seductive. To tell you the truth, I think it's a fable made up to lure people here because I haven't seen a single bloom. But then, I haven't strayed farther than this tower, and no one would let me wander if I tried.

At first, I wouldn't say I liked it, and I was lonely. Still, the Keeper brought me books and other necessities so that this enormous and octagonal chamber soon became as comfortable and cheerful as my rooms in our castle at Rosemyre. I haven't many visitors or friends, and I am not the sort of Princess who talks to animals or thinks that animals can talk to me. I've stuffed the mouse hole with rags to keep the nasty creatures in their place and not in mine.

Yes, I do like my tower. Except there is but one window. I suppose I should be happy about that. I could be locked in a dark room below the keep at Rosemyre, like my father and mother. I still have hope that they are alive. If they are not, I hope they're with the angels.

❧❧❧

THIS MORNING WHEN I woke, I sensed something new, something different.

It was silent except for the waves

crashing against the rocks below, the call of a gull. I slipped out of bed, climbed to the window, and was surprised to see boats riding the waves out to a ship well beyond the harbor. Only trading cogs came into port here. What fleet was this? The small craft was full of people, and waiting at the dock were not just the townspeople of Flowergate, but my household servants! My first thought was how brazen of them not to wake and dress me, let alone take the ship back to Rosemyre without me, for I was sure that was their destination.

Door slams startled me. I tumbled off the contraption and landed on my bottom. As I pulled myself up and cursed, I heard keys jangling, and that sound soon echoed in the tower, followed by excited chatter and giggles, even laughter.

Was The War over?

I was laughing and searching for my slippers and robe when Sir Eaelfred, my father's chancellor, entered after knocking on the door. He was dressed for either arriving or leaving, for his heavy cloak was fastened with a brooch around his barrel frame, and he held riding gloves in his hands. Sir Eaelfred's nose was perpetually red, like the color of apples, and it dripped as if he had a cold. His voice could put you to sleep; the low-pitched drone and gasping for air between words made conversation a struggle that wore one out. His bushy beard growing down past his chin made up for the sparse strands of hair tucked under his velvet cap. I noticed the absence of our family's device from the brim–an angel holding a great glowing rose.

"Eaelfred! Right trusty and beloved, we greet you well," I said, using my parents' formal royal greeting. My mother would be glad I hadn't forgotten the royal protocol. "You've come from Rosemyre? Are my parents well?" I now asked, running about and looking for clothes and shoes, my plain crown.

"Good morning, Prin . . . Lady . . . Ella," he greeted. Mumbled, rather. "I trust you slept well?"

"Lady Ella? Did you say, 'Lady Ella,' sir?"

"I, I did. Your . . . pardon, Lady."

"How is it that last night I fell to sleep Princess Eleanor of Rosemyre and this morning I am 'Lady Ella?'" I asked. My frown was more telling of my anger than the tone of my voice. My mother, the Queen, always said a princess should never betray her emotions. I waited patiently, and then, "Sir Eaelfred? Why will you not answer me? Why will you not look at me?"

Eaelfred sighed and did not look at me when he said, "My lady, you, ah, are no longer a . . . princess. The War is over. Their graces, the King, and Queen,"

"What about my mother and father?"

"They, they were taken from the castle at Rosemyre."

"Eaelfred, tell me they are not dead, nor executed!"

"They are banished . . . and have been placed on a ship. To, to the Greylands beyond the Sapphire Hills in the far north. Godrick Thorne said that he was the only man who could bring peace and make the kingdom as great as it was in the past when your great-grandfather Sigwulf reigned."

"How?" I barely spoke. "How did it end?"

"My lady, it is sorrowful. He took the princes' wives and children—"

"Stop! No more, please; I understand."

We lost The War; a quarrel no one alive could remember the why and how of it. It was finally over.

When Sir Eaelfred looked at me, I saw his tears, and immediately I regretted my anger. He has been my parents' friend and servant since before my birth. Before The War.

"Yet they did not take me. I shall not go to the Greylands." I considered this for a moment, and it then occurred to me. "Will they cut off my head?" I dared to ask.

"Your head—ah, I think not. You are to stay here at Flowergate until such a time as Godrick Thorne decides what's to be done," Eaelfred struggled with his words. ". . .with you. That is to say, where you will live, stay, a governess or guardian appointed until you come of age—your dowry. A husband found for you. Perhaps one of his sons."

I stood in the middle of the great room, hands folded before me in my most regal attitude, something my mother did in uncertain times. Raising my chin, I said, "We thank you for the news, however unhappy and undesirable it is. We will dress now. Please send for Bronwy."

"You will have to dress yourself, my lady. All of the household is gone or is going. By order of Thorne. It was a condition of sparing their lives that they leave immediately."

"God be praised; that is the first act of charity I've heard of where it concerns Thorne."

"There is one more."

Eaelfred pulled from his cloak a sealed scroll. He broke the seal and unfurled it before me on a table so that I might read the document. Before me was a treaty of some kind. My eyes blurred with tears as I recognized my father's handwriting and his signature. Rather than the familiar, firm, regular letters and rightward slant, the penmanship was irregular and jagged, as if the document was written under duress.

"He could not have sworn this oath willingly!" I whispered.

"He did. And for you, Lady. This accord guarantees that you will have the freedom to come and go as you please but only into the town and no further, and only if you swear not to escape Flowergate and only if you return to the castle by nightfall on the days you go out. You will be given an escort, of course,"

"Am I Thorne's hostage or not?"

"Of course you are, I mean to say, His Excellency Thorne wants your former subjects to see that he is not unkind to children, for he knows their love of you, and it will bode well for a future accord between the houses of Thorne and Willoughby when all of Rosemyre will be united as in the days of your father, our former King."

"Yet he has no qualm in locking up my parents."

"That is an unfortunate truth, I'm sorry to say, my lady. Unfortunate."

"And when I come of age, I'll be locked up. If I'm still alive."

"That is . . . well, prove that you are willing to obey in this and more freedoms will be granted, perhaps even a trip to the Greylands to see your parents."

Eaelfred took the quill from the inkwell on my writing table and handed it to me.

"I do this unwillingly. I do this to protect my parents," I said and carefully penned my name beneath my father's. That done, I assumed my regal pose and stared straight ahead and out the window. Once I glanced at Eaelfred as he nervously tucked the so-called accord under his cloak before he bowed and slipped quietly out of the chamber without my prompt. I can say by the look on his face we were both glad he was gone.

I kept my regal pose while considering what had happened—exiled in a town I'd never truly seen in a place no one wanted to visit. It could certainly be worse. And I could see my parents!

Godrick Thorne would find me an exemplary hostage.

With the poise and calm I'd seen in my mother, I sat before my desk and pulled towards me the large, heavy, book that contained my official calendar of appointments and tasks, the compendium of advice handed down from Queen to Princess for decades, illustrations of clothing and crowns, prayers, and proclamations.

The Great Book.

Item Number One: Dress Accordingly.

What did a former Princess wear?

I found my shoes under the bed and opened the chest where Bronwy stored my dresses. The tears didn't come until I knelt to choose what dress I would wear that day. It wouldn't be the cloth of gold. No one ever again would come to pay homage to Princess Eleanor of Rosemyre. At the bottom of the chest was the simple clothing worn for travel and Holy Week. There was no ornamentation, no decoration in gold and silver thread, just plain, simple, weaving in the cloth and dyed in shades of dark blue and plum. The colors would suit my less than brown, almost blonde hair and my sometimes gray, sometimes green eyes.

Dressed as I was and a single glance at my reflection in the windowpanes was proof I was no longer a princess. But neither was I a servant nor peasant. The face staring back at me wasn't tan from days outdoors in the sun, and I didn't have the 'mightier–than–thou' expression of a lady–in–waiting or the harried look of a pantry maid. Who was this girl of seventeen dressed in a plain gown and kirtle, an apron, and hair tied back with a shoelace? She was no one I knew.

At least I followed the instructions in the Great Book without error.

I have dressed accordingly.

Chapter 2

HOLLOW ECHOES THAT seemed to go on forever greeted me in each of the galleries and rooms I passed through; where once there had been comfortable but simple furnishings more suited for a merchant's house than this smallish castle, there were rags, empty chests, and overturned barrels. A cat was sleeping on the heavy table in the great feasting hall. It would take twelve men to cart it away.

The table, not the cat.

At least they left me both.

Tapestries, carpets, sideboards, chairs, pots, and pans. Everything worth a silver penny or more or wasn't broken was taken away by the servants when they fled.

I paused, a horrifying thought suddenly occurring to me, and then I turned on my heels and ran up a flight of stairs past the bower and into the small chapel. My gasp scared a mouse behind the altar, making it hurry back to its hole in the tiled floor. Just as I feared, not even our pretty chapel had been spared. The servants had taken everything but the fresco of Christ resurrected, and if they could have chipped away the paint, I'm sure they would have. The great crucifix was still suspended over the altar; it was too large and heavy to carry. The sanctuary lamp, the ruby eye of God, was too far above the altar to be snuffed out and stolen. It still burned. God was still present here.

On the floor to the right of the altar, I spied a candle someone missed in their looting. Taking the shawl from around my shoulders, I spread it on the bare altar and looked about for something to use as a candle stand. I used a shard of broken pottery found on the floor, pressed the unlit candle into the shard's unglazed side, and set it on the altar. As I knelt and offered prayers for my parents and our kingdom, the flame started from nothing to a blue glow and then to a bright orange spark in my mind's eye.

This evening when I returned for evening prayers, I would bring a flint and a Bible.

I WAS ALONE in my castle and tower
except for the occasional mouse and the
large cat, and the handful of guards left
when everyone else escaped. They looked
at me more with pity than interest, even
boredom. What was left that could be
used for ransom? My parents surely had
less than I. And if they wanted me for bed
sport, there were enough girls in the town
to satisfy those needs; I'd seen the pretty
lasses escorted into the castle precincts late
at night and hurried out at dawn. I knew I
was safe, for no one, not even the powerful
lords of Ugglesbarnby, who lived on the
moors beyond the Sapphire Hills, would
dare to contravene Godrick Thorne's word
or actions. He would not easily give up
this prize.

There was a knight called Harold who
always appeared whenever I entered a
room. He stood by and watched me clean
and tidy each of the rooms every day. I
never expected a visitor, but one could
always be surprised. Harold never offered
to help; he followed me like a quiet
shadow and only the ringing of his mail
coat, the creak of metal against leather, the

soft thud of booted footfall, let me know he was there.

One morning during my first month after the Accord, I woke and found Harold sitting on the landing outside the tower door.

"Good morning, sir," I greeted. "It's Harold, isn't it?"

He scrambled to his feet and bowed. "Surely it is, my lady."

"I'm going to town today. Will you accompany me?"

He frowned and was about to speak, and then, "Surely I will, my lady."

We went down into the donjon, the living quarters of the castle. Each room and gallery had been swept clean and decorated as best as I could manage, but there was one chamber I'd been avoiding, and that was the Audience Court. I had to pass through the pillared and arcaded hall to reach the donjon's main entrance that led out to the ward and fore gate and into town. Many happy hours were spent here with my parents on our occasional visits, and those memories came back as my eyes went to the bare plinth where we used to sit. Even the carpets were stripped off the wooden planks. The wall behind them showed mildew and stains where once the banners of Rosemyre and the great tapestries telling our ancestors' deeds hung proudly. Mother and I took the smaller thrones on either side of Father, and we wore our finest robes. These were crown-wearing days. I never complained about how heavy my small coronet was, but I always had a headache by the end of the ceremonies.

We'd witness diplomas, charters, and deeds; even I signed the bottom of the parchment and affixed my seal: a device showing me, Eleanor, seated on a throne with a lamb in my lap. I held an upright sword in one hand, a rose in the other. Around the edge of the seal were my name and title: Eleanor, Princess of Rosemyre, the Lady of the Greenhavens, and Keeper of The Sapphire Hills.

When foreign dignitaries came to this far corner of Rosemyre, I would attend audiences and feasts and be presented as my father's heir, for quite simply, I was. My brothers were killed in The War. No doubt some of these visitors to our kingdom looked me over as a prize to be bought for their unmarried princes. They wouldn't give me a second look now; I was sure of it.

Memories of Christmas and Easter Courts, of Name Day celebrations and tournament feasts, swirled around in my thoughts until it was too much to bear, and I struggled not to weep. With my head down so as not to see the court, I nearly ran and almost tripped on my skirts, came to a stumbling halt before the sentries at the great doors. They crossed their pikes against me and looked down at me with faces as blank as marble effigies. I tried a smile and then forced my most regal countenance.

"I wish to go out," I said. Was my voice haughty enough? The guards smiled back. "The noise from the street must be deafening; you did not hear me. I will go to town as I have been promised."

"Pardon, Miss. You're a hostage," said the taller and burlier of the sentries.

"I'm quite aware of my predicament. I will go to town. Move the pikes. Please."

"Being a hostage means being a prisoner, Miss," said the other, snickering.

"I said, I have permission."

"That's as you say," sniffed the first.

"Godrick Thorne has given me permission to come and go as I please so long as I remain in Flowergate. Now. If you would?"

"Now. I say you're a prisoner, and you're to do as you're told."

"Since I am the Lady of Flowergate, I give the orders. Move aside."

"As if you could make me, Miss!"

I pulled up a knee to strike where it would hurt most and prove how easy it would be to move him when I felt the hand on my shoulder. Harold had joined us and was shaking his head.

"Roger," said Harold, "move aside. It is as the lady says."

Knight and sentries stared each other down, and I was becoming more nervous. Would they truly keep me locked up here?

"I assure you, good men, I have no cause to run away. I have nowhere to go, do I?" I continued to press my case. "Godrick Thorne will judge you kindly, and who knows, perhaps an extra silver penny a month? A promotion in rank? I will speak on your behalf. What do you say?"

"If you don't come back, Godrick Thorne will punish your father or your mother, or both," the first sentry growled. "And then we'll punish *you*. Do *you* understand?"

He bent down and stuck his face close to mine, smiling insincerely.

"Perfectly. I will be a model of virtue. Harold will escort me and return me safely."

The sentries glanced at Harold and smirked. "And no doubt Harold will be a model of virtue," the first sentry jibed.

"A silver penny says I will," Harold replied, looking at the man straight in the eyes and with deadly intent.

The pikes were moved to allow passage.

"Good Sirs, I thank you." I tried a curtsey and nearly fell over; graceful movements were not one of my better qualities. Harold set me aright while the sentries pushed back the oak beam and threw their weight against the portals.

"Be back at sundown. Don't tarry," said the first sentry as I passed and walked out to freedom. Harold followed at a close distance but otherwise said and did nothing to impede my walk. When we reached the market square, he wandered off to a cook shop with the warning for me not to go anywhere but the market, or else.

Or else what? *Hah!* I could have easily run, but what surrounded me was more wonderful than freedom. It was a different kind of freedom. Oh, the sounds and smells, the many colors of the market square!

It was like a festival, this weekly occurrence. I'd never been to a market before, and now, wandering in and out of stalls and tents, listening to merchants extol the beauties, the flavors, the magnificence, of their wares, whether they be apples or amethysts, was a new experience and almost as extraordinary as receiving the Sacraments. Stalls covered with bright canopies of different colors, some painted with illustrations of their owners' wares, filled every space in the square so that it was an effort to walk, and soon being jostled and pushed by strangers was just part of the adventure. After an hour or two of exploration and walking freely, the scent of meat roasting and bread baking reminded my stomach that I'd not broken fast that morning, but I didn't care.

No one gave me a second thought. I was just another girl in a crowded, noisy, but wonderful place.

"*You're* in the way!"

The bark came from an old woman pushing a cart full of herbs and spices towards space at the square's end. I darted to my left and collided with a charcoal vendor, who apologized when I stumbled against his pushcart and knocked bricks of charcoal everywhere. He helped me back to standing.

The man's face was unremarkable; just another laborer dressed faded and twice-mended shabby clothes, with holes in his breeches and boots so worn that a dirty stockinged toe peeked through the top. But then he smiled, and his eyes lit like blue stars, and his face was creased with dimples, making him handsome.

"Now why haven't I seen you before?" the vendor said, watching as I swatted at my clothes to remove the charcoal dust. He smiled as I continued to make it worse with haphazard pats and swipes that only moved the dark smudges from one side of me to the other. What else could I do when I was used to having someone take care of these matters for me? I paid no attention to the women snickering behind their hands, and when I thought myself presentable, I smiled at them with all the confidence of a princess and asked one of the good wives for a loaf of bread and some cheese.

"Two and seven, Mistress Cindersoot," said the lady with her hand held out.

"What? No," I replied, "one loaf and one portion of cheese," my emphasis on the portions requested.

"Two and seven, Mistress!"

"Did I not just say—"

"That will cost you two silver pennies and seven coppers for one loaf of bread and one portion of cheese," the vendor interjected. He nodded towards my apron pocket.

I slipped a hand into the pocket and knew I'd come away with air. "I left my purse in the tower. Let me go and fetch my escort; if you would hold the bread and cheese for me, Good Wife?" I said sweetly and pointed towards the cook shop at the edge of the market.

"Why don't I bring it to your ladyship if it's all the same?" the lady replied.

"Would you? How kind and thoughtful, Good Wife!" I exclaimed though I didn't know at the time she was mocking me. The other women cackled like fowl at this and then started to shriek with laughter as I turned heel to find Harold. It was then I caught my reflection in a looking glass in one of the nearby stalls. Where was the respectable girl, the daughter of merchants I thought to make myself so I could fit in and get by while I waited for the summons from Thorne?

Somewhere under layers of dirt and soot.

This wasn't in the Great Book.

I was sure of it.

Chapter 3

 CLEAN RAG suddenly appeared before me, and I turned to see that the Charcoal Vendor offered it.

"My thanks, sir," I muttered and started dragging the cloth across my cheeks and brow, but all I did was make the smudges larger.

"I can fetch one of your ladies from the castle to help you, Mistress," he said.

"It wouldn't do any good; everyone's left, and I'm the only one—how did you know??"

"There's a reason they call ladies like you gentlewomen. You no more can wash that away than cinders and soot." The smile and eyes were kind, and he bent down to meet my gaze, which was fixed on two urchins chasing a goose. I was ignoring him while I considered three facts: one, I'd never chased anything; two, nor had I walked through a square on market day; and three, never, ever had I

talked to town folk. The Charcoal
Vendor's patronizing manner and gaze
only drew unwanted attention to those
truths.

"Your name, Mistress?" he now asked.

"Elea—Ella. I am Ella Cindersoot.
And you are—?"

He doffed his cap and bent himself into
an 'L' shape. More soot and ash fell as he
moved, and I darted out of their gray path.
"Ralph Falconer at your service, milady."

"No need for that!" I snapped. "You
wouldn't bow to a common girl."

"I would."

I stared at him in disbelief before trying
a curtsey of sorts. "Good day, sir; God
keep you safe."

As I nodded farewell, Ralph Falconer
stopped me with a coin he pressed into my
hand. "For your bread and cheese, Ella."

"I said, my escort has money, and I'm
going to get it. Thank you all the same."
The coin, a gold angel, caught the sun,
glinting. There were a few beggars who
looked over hungrily, waiting for their
chance to snatch it away as the precious
currency was held out carelessly.

"No, I beg you keep it. You never

know,"

Know what? I wondered as I slipped the coin into my apron pocket and went past the grumbling beggars to the cook shop.

Harold had no coins in his purse. He did have a half-eaten meat pie, a crust of bread, a bit of cheese, and an empty ale jug. He was dozy drunk with his head on the table.

"Harold!" I shouted at him. "Harold, wake up!" Tugging on his shoulder and yelling in his ears did no good. The shopkeeper came over, pried an empty cup from his hand, and took the jug and plate off the table.

"It's like this every time he comes in," the shopkeeper growled. "They ought to feed him and give him a bed up at the castle!" I was going to object but thought better of it. The shopkeeper smacked Harold across the face, and he was on his feet, swearing and reaching for his sword. "Someone's going to have to pay for what he owes. He's short a coin or two—doesn't have enough to pay for what he ate and drank, Miss."

Ralph Falconer's coin was in my apron pocket. I sighed and gave it over and, for my trouble, got a smile. It took some doing to get Harold out of the cook shop, but I managed and pushed him towards the castle.

I went home disappointed. There were no gold angels, silver pennies, or copper half-pennies in the secret wooden chest that lay in another wooden chest under the great table in the great hall. Both catches were pried and broken. Well, that was a secret no more. Besides, exiles and servants needed to eat, didn't they? Buy passage on a ship to some foreign land far away, where Godrick Thorne couldn't touch them? May that small fortune do them good.

The climb to my tower chamber used to be a game. Two steps and a faery hovering above the casement would give me a daisy; three steps, Holland tulips; ten would be a reward of lilies; twenty, a dozen roses, and by the time I reached the landing outside my door, I would have a marvelous bouquet with colors that clashed and scents that stirred the senses.

That afternoon, all I had were dried petals and weeds.

Once the door thudded and echoed to a

close, I stood in the middle of the chamber
and surveyed my tiny kingdom. I was
first struck by the bar of amber light on
the floor: dust motes sparkled like gold
dust, and their dance entertained for only a
moment. I looked about as if I should find
something to cheer me. Everything was
where I left it hours before. My needlework was draped on a rung of the stepping
stool to the window, and it was there I sat.
For the longest time I stared out of the
window and imagined that I was on one of
those boats riding the waves to the ship
bound for Rosemyre. No, I'd be sick to
my stomach and leaning over the bow.

With the loudest of sighs that disturbed
the dust motes, I picked up my needlework.

The sound of the needle and floss
pulling up and over the linen were
whispers of 'I-am-alone, 'I-am-alone,' as I
worked the pattern of knots and vines.
Once, this scarf for the buskin of a helmet
had been a name day gift for my father;
now I wasn't sure what it would be. I was
still pondering that when someone
knocked on the door. I paused, waiting.
Again, a knock.

"My lady?" Harold called.

"Enter!" I responded.

Harold bowed in greeting as he came in. In his arms was a wicker basket covered with a cloth. The scent of fresh-baked bread was irresistible, and my stomach began to rumble and growl.

"This was left for you at the market gate," Harold said as he placed the basket on a table and removed the cloth to reveal a feast of bread, cheese, apples, and sweet wafers. A small jug of ale was tucked into a corner of the basket, and wrapped in a rag were three silver pennies and two gold angels.

"Who would be so kind?" I wondered.

"A boy brought it; that is all I know."

"Surely not the good wives," I ventured. "It must be Ralph."

"My lady?"

"Nothing. Thank you; that is all."

Harold offered his courtesy, something like a nod of the chin and a weak smile, and slipped out—but not before I gave him an apple, and that seemed to cheer him up.

My supper that evening was a wafer and a drink of water. The basket lay untouched until the next morning when I could stave off hunger no more and took small portions to break my fast, for I didn't know from where or when another basket would appear at the market gate.

What I did know is that I had to make my way alone in the world.

Chapter 4

THE NEXT MORNING, I managed to dress quickly without my thumbs catching in the lacings of my kirtle or twisting off buttons. I even started a fire in the wall hearth over which I toasted bread and cheese. My thirst was slaked with water from the pitcher and a few sips of ale. I consulted the Great Book and tapped the entry with a finger. Morning Prayer. I didn't need a priest for that, but I did need a flint to light the candle.

Everything was as I left it on the day I learned The Terrible News, and when, after finishing my holy office and extinguishing the candle and watching the smoke rise to God, I turned and found Harold sitting in the back. He rose and nodded in greeting, then followed me out. He waited on the landing when I returned to my tower and consulted the Great Book for my daily tasks.

I practiced my penmanship and read

scripture aloud to improve my speaking voice, made a concise inventory of the gift basket, and marked them as 'done' in the Great Book. Harold didn't look the least bit annoyed by how I took my time. I think he enjoyed being away from the sentries. We repeated this pattern several days in a row until Harold spoke up on a particularly cold morning.

"Will we go to market today, Lady?" Harold asked hopefully. Our daily routine now included an excursion into town on market day and was usually Harold finding his way to a cook shop or alehouse while I explored the market.

I glanced up from my needlework and offered a smile, then returned to the pattern of rosebuds and vines on the hems of a shirt I'd made. Harold stepped forward and reached out, fingered the linen cloth, and then stepped away. "Beautiful work, Lady," he complimented.

"Thank you, Harold."

"My mother was a seamstress. She sold her work at the market. We were able to have food, an occasional sweet, and some coal for the fire."

"Where was your father?"

"Fighting in the war. He sent money home when he could. Pardon, Lady Ella, for speaking so informally."

I looked around in amusement, waving a hand and then smiling up at Harold. "Do you see any courtiers who might object? My parents? I do not think I hold court, nor is it expected, at least, not by the sentries." Now I started to fold the piece-work I'd made to keep myself busy. I wouldn't tell Harold that with each stitch, I silently prayed, needle down, '*God keep my parents safe,*' and needle up, '*Lord Jesus, make ours a kingdom of heaven.*' Sometimes I even prayed for myself.

Harold bowed away again, and this time he stood outside on the landing while I continued plying my needle. When the shirt was completed an hour later, I added it to my collection: folded and stacked on a shelf were tablecloths and kerchiefs I'd embroidered. Beside them were linen caps I'd sewn and stockings knit of the finest wool I'd unraveled from old shawls.

The rumbling of my stomach reminded me it was almost noon, and I wanted supper. The basket was empty. Sighing, I looked under the towel, hoping to have missed a wafer or apple slice. But there was none to be had. I had a few copper half-pennies in the little jar by the bed. An apple starting to turn was on the windowsill, and I hesitated before dropping it into my apron pocket. I'd save it for a moment of desperation if there was nothing else.

What to do, what to do . . .

Harold's recounting of his mother's industriousness came to mind, and I laughed in delight. I would take my needlework to a shop in the town and sell it!

I made sure to mark this in the Great Book under the category 'Industriousness and Independent Thought.'

There was only one seamstress I knew: Mistress Temby.

She came to the castle once a month with linens and new small clothes for me, though I rarely saw her, for she left her parcels at the kitchen door. Her work was exquisite, and I hoped she would see my needlework good enough to sell, even for a penny or two. Pennies added up and could purchase bread.

Harold wasn't in the stairwell when I

came out.

"Harold?" I called and waited for the echo to fade. "Harold! Harold, where are you? Where did you go?"

No one responded, and I waited another minute. Still, there was no answer to my calls.

I couldn't wait. I needed the custom, for I had no desire to starve to death in one of my father's castles. Aware of the threat to my parents, though, I left a note on my door:

> I am going to the shops. I will return
> no later than four of the clock; please
> leave my mother and father alone.
> Many thanks. Ella.

That would make them happy.

Not wishing to speak or deal with the sentries, I slipped out of the castle by the kitchen door and made my way to town, asking a gentleman leaving by the eastern gate where I might find the shop of a seamstress.

"Excuse me, sir! Do you know the town?" I asked, offering my brightest smile.

"That I do, Mistress," he said, pulling up rein and then doffing his cap.

"Where do the seamstresses and tailors keep their shops?"

"That would be Linengate," he said kindly.

"Where would I find it?"

"The covered street near the church. You'll see a sign. Linengate."

"Thank you! Good day!" I said. I didn't bother with a curtsey and waved goodbye as he set off.

His directions led me straight to an arcaded street near the church where dressmakers and cobblers had their shops. A sign with the word 'LINENGATE' in bold letters assured me I'd come to the right place. The shop windows displayed garments, boots, and shoes of every kind.

At the corner where Linengate became Coppergate—the street of pot smiths and ironmongers—two little children sat with their back against the wall of a shop, huddled together against the early winter gusts that were blowing down from the north. They looked away when I smiled and said good morning and pressed further against the wall, clutching a threadbare shawl around them. Their eyes were fearful and red-rimmed either from weeping or the cold. Surely they would be pretty babes with a bit of soap and water applied to their solemn faces.

"Good morrow," I greeted, crouched down to see them better and at their level. They said nothing and looked down, perhaps at their feet bound in rags. Those rags were muddy and as threadbare as the shawl.

I took the apple from my apron. "It's all I have for now, but I can purchase sugar buns if you'd like. The ones with berries." I next took a woolen shawl from my work basket. "This should do, don't you think?"

With gentle hands and a smile, I wrapped them in my shawl and made sure their feet were covered. I took out a linen scrap and wiped their faces gently. Yes, they were little cherubs, this boy and girl.

"What are your names? I'm Ella."

It was a while before they answered, the apple being passed back and forth between them. "I'm Olivia," said the girl in a thin voice. She nudged the little boy. "This here's my brother, Oliver."

"Where do you live?"

Again, they retreated against the wall,

this time hugging my shawl tighter. Oliver whispered rather loudly, "Don't tell her!"

"Now," I instructed, still smiling, "if your mother asks where you got this shawl and who gave you the apple, tell her Ella Cindersoot of Flowergate. Goodbye, Mistress. And you, good Master."

As I was walking away, Olivia called out, "Thank you, Miss! But Miss, Miss! We don't have a mother or a father!"

Stopping, I turned and went back. "Then be here when the clock in the church tower strikes and the shop keepers close up for the day. I have a place that's warm, and you can sleep there tonight. We can think of a place for you to live. Will you do that?"

"Yes!" they chirped.

"Do you know Mistress Temby?"

Olivia nodded. "She gives us bread and sometimes a blanket."

"Can you tell me where Mistress Temby keeps her shop?"

"Just there," said Olivia, pointing up the lane.

"I'll see you later, then?"

"Goodbye, Miss! Bless you!" they

called out.

I could have sworn I saw Ralph Falconer at the edge of the market, smiling, as I walked to Mistress Temby's shop.

⟨✦⟩

A GIRL LOOKED up when I entered and said 'Hello.' She smiled shyly and put down her work to come to the counter that divided the shop into two rooms: a waiting area and a workroom. "Is there something you want, Miss?" she asked, dipping in a perfect curtsey. My governess Lady Pratt would have been ecstatic. As you have seen, I always look like I am ready to topple over when I curtsey, which I nearly did when I tried to return the greeting. The girl helped me upright and frowned at me in concern.

"You're so pale!" she exclaimed. "And thin!"

"It's no matter; I only just broke my fast. Thank you for your concern."

"But you're so pale, Mistress! Surely you'll swoon in a faint!"

How could I tell her I seldom went out of doors and that was the reason for my pale skin; that princesses were supposed to be ghostly pale because it was the fashion?

"If you have some water, then," I suggested.

"Would you like a cup of Sally's milk? It's fresh."

I assumed correctly that Sally was a cow or goat, for the girl led me to the back of the shop and out onto a patch where a goat was tethered to a withering apple tree, and there was a shed from which she brought a bowl of milk. It was sweet, warm, and welcome. I wiped my lip on my hand and smiled back at the girl. "I'm looking for employment," I finally said. "That's why I came here. I am good with a needle and can take piece work or mending for a half-penny." My needle-work came from the basket, and the girl gasped.

"How lovely! You do fine work. This is worth more, Lady! I swear it!"

"Is it? Thank you. Would you be able to sell it?"

"Would you be willing?"

"Of course; my family," I hesitated and then said, "my family is gone. The War took them."

"May God assoil them!" she said,

crossing herself. "I lost an uncle."

"May God assoil him."

We looked at one another, recognizing the pain of loss that often made a bond. The girl patted my hand solicitously, and we went back to the shop.

It was a bright, neatly kept, and colorful place where the latest fashions in the Kingdom were on display. I smiled when I saw an excellent copy of my mother's Christmas Revels gown and my own Easter gown and cap.

"Is Mistress Tenby about?" I queried. "It is she I've come to speak with."

"Any moment now, Mistress. She's been to mass."

While I waited, the girl stitched together the sleeve and bodice of a woman's kirtle. Her needle flashed in the sunlight and swiftly moved through layers of fabric. Here I thought no one was quicker and neater in their work than me and this girl proved she was ten times ten better. The sleeve was attached to the kirtle and the other sleeve pinned when the door opened and the proprietress, Mistress Temby, entered.

The girl leapt to her feet and curtseyed;

I stayed where I was. Nervously the girl whispered, "Get up! Get up! It's the mistress!" But there was no need to offer my respect, for Mistress Tenby gaped at me with bugged-out eyes and exclaimed, "Princess Eleanor!" She prostrated herself before her bewildered assistant and me.

Chapter 5

"I PRAY YOU get up, Mistress Temby. I am Ella."

I took her arm and she rose swiftly, which was surprising, given her age and the elaborate kirtle she wore. The seamstress went a shade of scarlet when our glances met. "Why would you call yourself that?" she asked, managing a smile.

"I'm sure you know why," I murmured, glancing at the girl, who smiled, and I knew for certain she was pretending not to notice for twice she pricked a finger with her needle.

"I'm positive I don't," she replied in a tearful voice.

"The War is over," I whispered. "The King and Queen were sent into exile, and I am a surety of their good faith not to return, at least, that's what I've put together of the explanation given to me." In a louder voice, I said, "I see that you mistake me for the late Princess Eleanor. I've been told that we resemble one another."

Mistress Temby patted my hand sympathetically as if I was a daughter or friend, and I didn't mind. I was neither and had none. "The poor dear! What a sweet and kind lady she was, Princess Eleanor." she crooned. "All alone in that castle, with no family or friends. Well, whatever her fate, she is happier, I am sure. Now, mistress! What do you require? A bonnet? A woolen kirtle of forest green? That would suit your coloring."

"I have talent with needle and thread, and I would be glad of some piecework," I answered truthfully and was surprised at how easily the words tumbled out of my mouth.

"She's clever with a needle, Mistress," the girl said, watching us closely.

"Then I shall have two clever girls and hopefully one that doesn't bleed on new silk!" Mistress Temby pronounced as she watched the girl suck at her thumb. She crooked a finger at me, saying, "I will show you the stores. The best flosses and bolts of cloth, buttons of every kind! Now come,"

I followed her through a door and down to a cellar with shelves that rose from floor to rafters and carried everything imaginable for a seamstress.

"We are alone, my lady," the Mistress said as she pulled spools of floss and squares of linen and placed them in my hands. "You still haven't told me why you call yourself Ella."

"Princess Eleanor is the heiress of Rose-myre, The Greenhavens, and Keeper of The Sapphire Hills. Ella Cindersoot is no one."

Mistress Tenby nodded after studying my face, and I noticed tears in her eyes. "Ella Cindersoot is my semptress if anyone asks, and I'll give you an angel for what you have in the basket and a silver penny a week—and an angel for special commissions. What do you say?"

⚜

WITH THAT ASSERTION, my new life began to look hopeful. I returned to the castle with a basket of piecework: a bonnet for a child, a shirt to be mended, a night shift to be embroidered at the neck and hems. I also brought Olivia and Oliver home, purchased several bread rolls, sugar buns with berries, some cheese, apples, dried venison, and cow's milk with the money earned from the sale of my needlework. I spread a meal at the kitchen table with this bounty and bade them sit.

How strange that I should enjoy watching another eat, and it was even more delightful to see how their faces glowed, their bodies relax as they grew comfortable in my company, and their stomachs full. When Oliver started to nod, I looked about and saw the open door to the pantry. This would be the best place for the children as there was no furniture in the bedchambers and no fires in the hearths. It was no surprise to find the empty shelves and barrels. My servants left me empty sacks tossed on the floor. When I started to fold them one on top of the other, Olivia jumped up to help me, and we made a bed of the sacks and the shawl.

"Are you a queen, Mistress?" Olivia asked. "Only queens live in castles like this."

"I was a companion to the queen, and

now that she's gone away, I live alone," I answered. Olivia began an inquisition while I stoked the fire in the kitchen hearth, and she tucked in beside her little brother.

"Do you miss the queen?" she asked.

"Very much. She was a kind lady."

"Do you have a mother and father?"

"Yes," I answered and was about to say that they were dead but stopped myself. I smoothed the hair out of Olivia's face and kissed her cheek. "You shall live better than I; I'm going to find a proper home for you. Perhaps with the sisters at St. Swithin's Under Wormhill? They will give you warm clothes, teach you to read, and cipher numbers. You'll have a warm bed every night, and you'll have good porridge and apples every day," I said.

"Why can't we live here with you??"

"I'm only here for a little while. It wouldn't be fair."

"What about you, Mistress Ella? Where will you go?"

"I shall find my way, I'm sure."

"I'll pray for you."

"And I you. Good night, Olivia."

"Good night!"

"Lady Ella!" Harold called to me when I was leaving the kitchen. I stopped and waited. He sauntered up and handed me the note. "It's a good thing I know how to read. Don't do that again. I don't think you're worth the trouble."

"I'll remember that!" I snapped.

Up the stairs I went to my tower.

This time when I reached the tower door, I had a small bouquet of pale flowers.

And two snowy white owls.

Chapter 6

IN MY PAST life, court activities counted the changing of the seasons and time, from the Christmas Revels to Harvest Ball. In Mistress Temby's shop, time was marked by the clothing we sewed and just by looking out the window. This winter was the coldest people could remember. I never knew how cold it could be with snow on the ground and me without a fur-lined cloak. I saw that the tower and castle were warm with fires lit day and night, but out in the streets of Flowergate, it was freezing. After I met Olivia and Oliver, I paid more notice to the poor folk, especially the children in the town, and for that reason, I began to knit for them.

"Ella, what are these?"

Mistress Temby's girl, whose name was Ariella, uncovered the basket I'd brought in that morning and found a stack of little caps, mittens, shawls, and cloaks.

"For the children. The little ones out in the street and market. They have nothing to keep them warm," I said, undraping the Christmas Revels dress I was making for a noblewoman in town, one Lady Ferrett.

"Where are the lace gloves for Mistress Alnwick?" Ariella asked.

"In the basket, beneath the shawls," I replied, my mouth full of pins as I hemmed the over-gown so that the pale blue would show, like a reflection on the ice of a pond. It was my first design and independent work, and I was anxious to finish it.

"Did the Mistress ask for these?"

"She did not. I thought of it myself."

"For the children?"

"For the children."

"Ah."

A disapproving sigh if ever there was. As Mistress Temby gave me more responsibility and finer piecework, our friendship waned. Ariella started eyeing me with suspicion. She spoke to me only when necessary and tried to disparage me before the Mistress. There wasn't an hour of the day that she didn't remind me of who I was: Ella Cindersoot, the orphan girl, the girl who came asking for piece-work for pennies.

"She'll not take kindly to wasting your time on street rats when you should be taking care of custom that pays, Ella Cindersoot," Ariella sniffed.

"I think she might," I replied, and Ariella was ready to swoop down from her ladder and pounce when the shop door opened, and a regal woman and young gentleman entered, paused, and looked about. The woman looked as if she was smelling something from the gutter; he looked sleepy. She was elegant and dressed far better than any lady I'd seen at my parents' court.

An emerald could not have been as bright green nor as shimmering as her kirtle and over-gown of sarcenet silk shot with gold thread. The veil covering her snowy hair was so delicate in weave one might think spider webs had been used to create it; from the hems of this veil dangled diamonds and emeralds. All of this made you dismiss her plain, horsey features.

The young gentleman—well, what can I say? He was golden, blue-eyed, handsome with a squared jaw and dimpled cheeks, with rosy color in his tanned face—and sleepy, judging by his yawns and the continual shaking of his head to wake himself.

"What do you require, my lady?" Ariella asked, dipping in a graceful curtsey that made me envious. "Mistress Temby is ever ready to serve."

"Thomas," the lady called and snapped her fingers for a servant that appeared from the street. In his hands was a parcel wrapped in velvet, which he presented to her with an 'L'-shaped bow. She carefully unfolded it to reveal a fine garter with a golden buckle. The motto had been damaged, and many letters were missing.

"Can you read, mistress?" the lady asked Ariella, who flushed with color and touching the embroidered letters with a finger hesitated, and then said, "'Long live the king-?'"

"Long live-? It is hardly that! You, girl! Yes, you. Come here."

I didn't bother to curtsey but nodded and came forward, taking pins out of my mouth. I smiled, glancing first at the lady, then the young gentleman, who seemed to wake up when I smiled at him.

"My lady?" I asked.

"Can *you* read?"

I studied the motto and then nodded. I'd seen this before. My father and the knights sworn to him wore them on holy days and for the Great Council meetings. Surreptitiously I glanced at the young man.

"If I'm not mistaken, it says 'God Give Blessing and Honor to Those Who Serve the True King,' I said and nodded again. "I believe it says that."

"Precisely! Well, I've traversed the region looking for a seamstress who can read. But can you mend and sew? Will you repair this? A hunting accident ruined the lettering. It is needed for the Prince's twenty-first birthday," the lady said.

I was ready to reply when I noticed the young gentleman was wide awake and smiling at me.

"And when might that be?" Ariella interrupted.

"A fortnight and six days. Can it be done?" the lady demanded.

"What's this?" asked Mistress Temby when she entered from the back of the shop with an armful of dresses for display.

"Mistress, this ornament needs repair," Ariella said. "There are letters embroidered in gold, and it looks like jewels are missing."

"Let me see . . . ah! The Garter Royal of Rosemyre! Only sworn knights have this honor," the Mistress said. She smiled at the woman. "We shall do all that you require, my lady. My semptress Ella, here, will see to it." She pushed me forward gently. "May I inquire as to your ladyship's name?"

"I am Esmerelda, Duchess of Prowde in the Principality of Worthy."

"Your ladyship," Mistress Temby simpered as we all three curtseyed. I managed to tumble onto my bottom, and the young gentleman was speedy in his response and willing to help me to my feet. We smiled at one another for the longest time.

Ariella scowled as the precious garter was placed in my keeping and the young gentleman gave whispered thanks as he departed, smiling, and did I mention, wide awake?

I WENT HOME that afternoon the happiest I'd been in months. I didn't even care that Harold was drunker than usual and sang a bawdy song as we picked our way through the market square. Ralph Falconer bowed when we passed, and I could have sworn he winked at me. His blue eyes were glowing in a face powdered by soot.

The crones in the market no longer teased me; they ignored me as I learned to say nothing in response to their hurtful comments and cruelty.

To many in Flowergate, I was the Shop Girl. Having arrived in the dead of night three years ago and never going outside the castle until recently, no one knew me as anyone else.

I was thriving yet still worried and preoccupied. There wasn't a day I didn't think of my parents and wonder about them. If I was clever enough, I could send a message to my parents to tell them that all would be well and that I was well. Olivia and Oliver thrived on the attention I gave them, but I knew they needed better care than I could offer.

Several weeks later, I woke on a

Sunday morning in excellent humor, for I had a plan. First, I would bring the children to the sisters at St. Swithin's Under Wormhill and pay for their keeping; that way, they would receive an education and wouldn't have to live on the street. Oh, that I could do so for every child in Flowergate!

"But why must we go?" Oliver whined as we walked along the path through the lychgate and into the abbey precincts.

"You don't listen!" Olivia snapped at her younger brother. She tossed her dark braids back and glared at him, adding, "It's only for a little while. When Mistress Ella can buy a house on the market square. Then we shall live with her again."

"Precisely, Olivia," I said. "The sisters will give you lessons in reading and writing and doing ciphers with numbers. You can have your own shop when the time comes. And you, Oliver, might be esquired to a knight and learn chivalry."

"I have a gift for you, Mistress," Olivia said as she reached into the sack that carried her change of clothes and the needlework I'd taught her. A square of rough wool was pulled out, and I saw a pretty embroidery of two owls on an oak branch. "To remember us."

We hugged one another at the abbey doors, and I almost wept as the abbess took Oliver and Olivia's hands and walked with them, speaking quietly to the children as they rounded a corner to where the guesthouses stood.

I returned home in a darker mood. It was the proper thing to do, leaving the children in the safekeeping of the good sisters of St. Swithin's Under Wormhill. I knew they were charitable and knew several successful merchants in Flowergate benefited from their schooling and nurturing. Still, I had given up two friends.

While packing up a basket of finished piecework and wrapping the precious garter royal with silk flosses and packets of replacement jewels in a woolen shawl, I felt a little downcast but knew I was left with no other tragedies.

Oh, how I hated it when I was wrong!

Chapter 7

I CIPHERED THAT it would take another three days to mend the garter if that was the only work I had. Mistress Temby made that possible, much to Ariella's dismay. When she complained about the unfairness of it, the mistress reminded her that the income from this commission would be substantial and bring in a better, more valuable, custom and perhaps the Christmas bonus of an angel.

"Now there's the look of a cat that got the cream," remarked Ralph Falconer when I strolled through the market after the end of the day. All I had in my basket was the garter and was looking forward to the evening when I could sit in my tower and continue mending the letters and applying jewels.

"How was your custom today, Master Falconer?" I greeted, stopping by.

"The snow will come soon; I'm doing a

fair trade. And you?"

"Well enough. Good evening, sir. I must be back by sundown—there's my escort now."

Ralph tugged the brim of his cap and winked as I started out, and he grinned when I suddenly spun about and came back.

"Master Falconer, do you have custom in the Greylands?" I asked.

"I do, Lady Ella,"

"And do you go there often?"

"Not very, but there are men who travel for me."

"Would you," I took a sealed letter out of my basket and put it on the counter. "take this to Bramble Court?"

"The castle?"

"Yes, just so."

Ralph glanced around as if worried we were being spied upon and then frowned. "I know a man who would for a silver penny or two."

"I couldn't trust him. But I trust you, sir," I admitted.

The letter was pocketed, and Ralph smiled again. "I'll see what I can do."

We parted at that and none too soon for

Harold staggered from the cook shop barking that he wouldn't be accountable for my disobeying orders.

"Your life isn't worth my losing bed and board, Lady Ella," Harold complained as we walked back.

"I am your Princess and no doubt your Sovereign!" I muttered and was glad he didn't hear me for the shouting from the sentries as we approached just as the bells were ringing curfew. Once inside, I was brought to the audience court, where Eaelfred waited, pacing back and forth until he saw me and bowed in greeting.

"Where have you been, Lady? I've been waiting an hour!"

"Is it my parents, Eaelfred? Tell me it isn't!" I demanded, dropping my shawl and basket where I stood and sank to the floor.

"I could say it is, but that is dependent on you," Eaelfred sighed.

"Then what?" I begged.

"Tell me now. Did you encounter a lady and gentleman in town?" he asked. "A young prince and his governess?"

My eyes slid to the basket and the garter royal sticking out from under a linen towel. "They asked Mistress Temby to repair a garter—the commission was given to me." And here I produced the garter and showed it to Eaelfred, whose eyes bugged out at the sight of it.

"Where did they get this? Only your Father can bestow—my lady, do you know?" Eaelfred gasped, seizing the garter.

"How should I, Eaelfred?"

"You are to return it at once! If Godrick Thorne hears about this, your life would be in danger, and no doubt you'd be taken away to the Greylands!"

"I wouldn't know where to return the garter. They gave me a fortnight and some days to make the repairs. I assume that means they'll be coming by to claim it."

He thrust the garter at me. "Return it to the shop tomorrow. And you mustn't go there again."

"But-!"

"What is more important to you, my lady? A pastime or your parents' lives?"

"It is not a pastime! How do you think I've managed to buy food and kindling? To get new small clothes and stockings? To clothe the poor children of Flowergate when no one else will bother? It is no pastime, sir, but my living!" I argued passionately.

"It won't mean anything if you haven't got a life!" Eaelfred barked. "See to it, Eleanor Willoughby!"

The unaccustomed anger did not surprise me, but his use of my name: my real, Christian, name.

That night I put aside my needlework and took up my prayer beads. Buried under the coverlets with the cat on the pillow beside me, I whispered *Pater Nosters* and Hail Maries. I prayed for my mother, my father, and myself, for Olivia and Oliver. I thought of the sleepy prince, especially his deep, sparkling blue eyes that smiled—if eyes could smile—when we first greeted one another and when he helped me off the floor. His whispered thanks and smile as he left with the Duchess of Prowde. I dreamed of riding across the moors beyond the Caves of Wormhill and stopping by a great, ancient, oak tree, where we kissed and embraced and swore undying, unassailable, love to one another.

Oh, that anything cruel might happen

to him because of my willingness to please!

When morning came, I hurried out of the castle without Harold, slipping out through the kitchen door when I knew the sentries would be sleeping or passed-out drunk. The market square was coming to life when I arrived and headed for Mistress Temby's shop where I would relinquish the garter and run back home before anyone would miss me...

Terwit, terwit.

The whistling startled me, and I looked around for a dog or a horse loose in the market. Then I saw Ralph Falconer, who was gesturing wildly. People about their business jostled me back and forth as I tried to reach him, and when I finally arrived at his stall, he pulled me into the cramped space and slammed the counter so that we were crouched in a dark box that stank of burnt wood and earth and other disgusting, earthy things. Something brushed my leg, but I didn't dare look; I knew we would be discovered if I screamed. Ralph Falconer whispered something I couldn't make out, but it sounded by his anxious sound as if something awful was afoot. Steadying myself by grabbing what I hoped was a charcoal log, I waited until my sight adjusted to the dimness and looked to where I believed he knelt.

"What are you about?" I demanded.

"You should not have come to town today," Ralph whispered. "Soldiers arrived a moment ago. Have they been to the castle?"

I suddenly felt cold, and then a sweat started in my armpits and on my face. That sick, breathless sensation of fear took over, and for a moment, I couldn't hear what Ralph was telling me. He grabbed my hand, and we crawled out of the stall by a small hatch facing away from the market. When we came out, we were at the perimeter and behind a pig seller's stall. Bracken and grass obscured us, and the pigs were an excellent shield against two knights that were talking to a cobbler nearby. They wore the raven encircled by a red crown of thorns on their tabards. Off on the horizon, I saw the sails of a ship in the harbor that carried the same device.

Godrick Thorne!

"Princess Eleanor, I am ever ready to serve you," Ralph said.

There was no use in pretending to be shocked at his comment. "Am I so bad at pretending?" I asked.

"No, as I said, you couldn't wash away your nobility with soap and water."

"But you knew who I was and let me play a foolish game!"

"Not until you appeared at the market. I added two and two and got a princess who'd never been on her own before. And that's a very, very, dangerous state to be in."

"What should I do?" I croaked in a whisper.

"Get away from Flowergate as quickly as you can."

"I know a carpenter in Sullen, and I know the abbess at St. Swithin's Under Wormhill. Perhaps the soldiers won't go there?"

"Well, I'd go to Sneaton and Ruswarp. It's far enough inland—by the time they sailed that far north and marched to the west, you'd be out of their reach. I can take you."

"You won't risk your life for me! I can

take the forest paths and follow along the Caves at Wormhill to get that far west."

"I don't doubt it, Princess. And will you use your gentle manners on the wolves and brigands that hide in the forest?"

My argument was swallowed with the lump in my throat.

Then we were racing through alleys and streets back to the castle. Fear kept me from crying out when we approached the gates. Riding away and within our sight were the lady and young gentleman from Mistress Temby's shop.

What were they doing at the castle?

"Wait here," I whispered to Ralph, and I took off before he could catch me up. The kitchen door was unlocked as I knew it would be, and I gained entry without being seen, for the sentries were gone, as was Harold. Of course they would save their hides before mine! And here I thought Harold was a friend and my guardian! If ever we met, I would sort him out...

The cat was sleeping on the landing outside my chamber door. It stretched languorously and meowed when I stumbled over him. While I was gathering up all that I could into a sailcloth sack, I heard horses and soldiers. There was no time to climb onto the platform to see who it was. I knew. Before I left the tower chamber, I espied the Great Book. I wasted only a moment to stuff it into the sack as best I could.

I scrambled down to where Ralph waited for me outside.

"They've come! We have to go now!" Ralph whispered.

"I know."

"That was foolish—leaving me like that!" he grumbled.

"It doesn't matter now, does it? Besides, everyone is gone."

I didn't look back for a last, tearful gaze at my home of three years. When Ralph saw how I dragged the sack carrying my belongings and food, he took it from me and hefted it over his shoulder as if it was a dishcloth.

"Something is wrong. Well, of course something is wrong, but I don't understand, and yet I do," I whined, struggling to keep up. "No one was there, and nothing was touched. Did they all go over to Godrick Thorne? Did they betray me—and what kind of soldiers are these that don't loot or kill?!"

"A princess is the real coin to a man of state and his knights," Ralph explained as we hurried away. "She is the true prize. No doubt they had orders to take only you for whatever reward was offered, or they were paid to leave you helpless. I think it the last."

"I can't believe that Harold betrayed me and left me at the mercy of Thorne,"

"Here—this is the safest route."

Ralph pointed toward a clearing that led into the West Woods, and we ambled and tripped over uneven ground made more perilous by rocks that seemed to appear from nowhere and pitches of grass and moss hiding gullies, sometimes trenches. After a while, I didn't mind, for it seemed I traveled faster when I tumbled or tripped. My landing spot always pointed me towards the woods.

We didn't pause until the path into the woods stopped at an enormous oak. It was one of those monstrosities with trunk and branches the sizes of grown men and always a cleft in the trunk where a person could take shelter, and the canopy stretched for yards so that the sun and the land surrounding it was obscured in an ever-present twilight.

"Only a moment," Ralph panted as he looked about to see if we were followed. I knew he meant it would be a quick respite and leaned against the tree to catch my breath and take inventory of bruises and cuts.

"I thank you, sir," I finally spoke up. "Why do you help me? If I am the true prize, why did you not hand me over to Thorne's men? You'd have a living for a year or more."

Ralph gave me a sideways glance—one of those grimaces prefaced by a silent 'I-Can't-Believe-You-Sorted-It-Out' look.

"I had it in mind, Princess. That's the truth of it. But a promise to the King held more weight. And more gold."

"My father?"

"Before his exile, my lady. He asked me to protect the girl in the castle if anything should happen and to get you away from Flowergate if necessary."

I was ready to scoff at his self-importance and tell him to keep his

dreams to himself when I remembered
that the Lord God used a shepherd boy and
a carpenter's son to do His work. A king
might use a diplomat or a knight or a
charcoal vendor.

"If ever I meet my father again, I will
commend you to him," I said.

"My thanks, Lady."

The awkwardness of the revelation was
relieved when Ralph nodded towards the
woods, and we spent the rest of the day
moving further and further from the
eastern coast of my father's kingdom until
forest gave way to the caves and patches of
forest at Wormhill. At nightfall, we
found a cave and tucked in until dawn the
next day. I drifted off to the sound of
nature: the wind in the trees and
hedgerows, the hooting of owls.

Exhaustion made it easier to sleep.

Chapter 8

I WOKE WITH a knot in my stomach—not from hunger—it was the realization I was someone's prey, and it would be a folly to camp here longer than necessary. Ralph dropped a fur-lined cloak over me sometime during the night, for I was warm and comfortable despite the hard earth of the cave that was my bed. My eyesight adjusted to the morning sun shining into the mouth of the cave, and I studied the patterns of stone of lichen on the walls, took in the good, damp scent of moss and earth, listened to morning. I was safe in Creation.

I thought I was the first to rise, but when I went out and looked about for a place to deal with my water, I saw Ralph stripped to the waist and washing in a clear pond. Not knowing much of the world and certainly not of men, I saw the stripes across his back and chest before noticing the man's fine form. The stripes were different faded colors of red and brown; they were the irregular scars of a lashing. His muscular form and the slightly larger right arm made me think he was a knight. A proven knight. There were strange knots on his shoulder blades where it looked as if the bones had been broken and mis-set. Ralph turned at the sound of my footfall and bowed, grabbing his shirt at the same time.

"You might have said you were a knight," I greeted. "I would have been more cordial."

"The fact is, I'm not. But you should be cordial in any case," he replied.

"You sound like my father."

"I've known your father since before you were born."

"You're not that old." Then, "Where did you get the cloak?"

"Does it matter?"

"Thank you."

"You're welcome."

"Who are you, Ralph Falconer? Who are you really?"

"Let's save this for another morning, my lady. We have a day's walk before we reach Sneaton and Ruswarp. You won't be safe until then."

"Which is it?" I asked.

"Your pardon, Lady?"

"Where shall we go?" I said. "Sneaton or Ruswarp?"

"Ah! It's one town. Two hamlets that converged in the days of your grandfather. You'll find it pleasant enough. Now let's be on,"

My hopes of pleasant conversation were dashed as we traversed the western gorse and heather-marked countryside through the valleys and high moors. Ralph Falconer walked a pace ahead of me and said nothing until we reached the gates of Sneaton and Ruswarp at dusk.

There were no sentries to bar our entry, just a steady stream of country and hamlet folk leaving the town after a market day. We picked our way through the lines; just two more travelers come to find beds for the night and bread and ale.

Off to the right of the market cross was a splendid building that looked like a manor house with fresh timbering and plaster and a door painted blue with iron hinges in the shapes of vines and flowers. Windows were lit, and the sounds of conversation and lively music were lures for a traveler. The wooden sign dangling from the eves proclaimed it to be The Angel and Virgin. I took a few steps in its direction, but Ralph held me back. "We go here, my Lady."

He led me towards a shop on the other side of the square. It was another pretty place, with ivy climbing the walls and flowering vines tracing a green door. A single lamp lit the entrance, and when Ralph knocked twice, another light flickered like a firefly, and its brightness blinded us when the door opened rather quickly.

A grandmother with plump, unblemished, rosy cheeks and what looked to be round brown eyes smiled at us, a question on her lips that turned into a squeal of delight when she saw Ralph. She was quite engaging, and I immediately felt safe in her presence.

"Master Falconer!" she exclaimed with joy. "You did keep your promise!"

"Mother Winifred, it is indeed a joy to see you once again. As you say, I did keep my promise, and here is your new seamstress, Mistress Ella Cindersoot, a

Shop Girl of Flowergate."

I made my usual awkward curtsey—
and prevented from tumbling over by
Ralph. It was then I saw she held a shawl
with my needlework bordering the hems.
As much as I wanted to touch the soft
woolen fabric and ask how she came to
possess it, I remembered this was a strange
place, and she was a stranger. Thus, I
nodded demurely in greeting, then looked
at Ralph, who smiled at Mother Winifred.

"You are welcome, most welcome, my
lady!" Mother Winifred crooned, and she
gently pulled me into a well-appointed
sitting room on the second floor of the
shop. I wanted to take a better gauge of
my surroundings and, apparently, my new
home, but she moved so quickly that I
found myself sitting on a comfortable
bench before a wall hearth.

"I beg your pardon, Mistress," I said
when she handed me a cup of brandywine
and a sweet wafer. "I am Ella Cindersoot,
a Shop Girl from Flowergate. I am no
lady."

"We'll take care of that!" she replied,
winking.

Of the rest of the evening my recollection was hazy at best, for soon I found myself lulled to sleep by the sound of whispered conversation and argument, the slam of a door, and heavy footsteps.

I woke in the morning to find myself in a pretty room that looked like my tower apartment, only brighter and with a second window. What could have been more surprising than waking after a pleasant sleep with all my treasures and pastimes available to me? I was settled on the topmost floor of a three-storied house and shop that soon held more surprises.

Mother Winifred saw to my happiness as well as my needs. My chamber had a chapel, of all things. It was more like a closet for its depth and narrow width, but a prayer desk was set with an illuminated book of Gospels, some prayer beads, and a tiny altar upon which sat a lovely Virgin and Child icon and a carved, wooden cross. A sanctuary lamp shone its ruby eye from the timbered and plastered ceiling. From that ceiling, two angels and two owls smiled down at me. It became my discipline to kneel before the altar every morning at waking and before sleeping to pray and offer my repetitive petitions for my parents and our kingdom. To these, I added the safety of Olivia and Oliver, the sleepy young gentleman and, strangely enough, Harold.

Another familiar routine was that no sooner had I finished my prayers than Ralph Falconer would knock at the door and invite me downstairs to break fast with him and Mother Winifred. We would enjoy the first meal of the day, and afterward, he disappeared into the streets of Sneaton and Ruswarp for hours and not return until after dark when he bade me sweet dreams before I slept.

In between these times, I worked in the shop and was soon familiar with the town's great and small. The tinker who needed his stocking mended received the same attention and courtesy as Lady Tode, Sneaton and Ruswarp's only nobility. Few could say where and when she received her title and from which great family she came, but she received respect and courtesy and was very kind and pleasant. The tinker, Master Moorehead, was a widower with an appearance as gruff as his voice and of few words or smiles. Lady Tode was a tall, elegant woman with eyes the color of steel and hair as black as jet beads. She was beautiful for a woman of advanced years, for the only clue to her age was the fine map of lines across her brow and around her mouth and eyes. Her mouth drooped just a bit so that it looked as if she could do nothing but scowl. Her manner and deportment were calm, though she tended to be flustered and forgetful, and for this she had a lady-in-waiting named Clara, who always had the right thing to say at the right moment. It happened that Lady Tode and Master Moorhead came to the shop at the same time of day, every day.

"Another hole." Master Moorehead held up a pair of stockings that showed two enormous holes at the toe and heel in each. "My best pair."

"We shall fix you up right away, Master Moorehead. Is tomorrow soon enough?" Mother Winifred chirped happily as his stockings were placed on the counter between them, and he walked out, nodding 'hello' and 'goodbye' to Lady Tode as she swooped in with Clara. Before she could be asked her pleasure, Lady Tode said, "My dears, it is not to be believed! His Excellency Thorne is coming to Sneaton and Ruswarp! He is making a royal progress and will hold Christmas Revels in the Guild House!"

"Can this be so?" Mother Winifred said, a smile frozen in place.

"I shall need a new gown, as will my girl here. His Excellency Thorne has invited all his subjects from Flowergate to the Sapphire Hills to celebrate his victory over the Willoughbys."

"Ah!" Mother Winifred replied, that smile still frozen.

"And you, pretty mistress," Lady Tode said to me, "of course you will go. I do not doubt there'll be plenty of handsome young men looking for dancing partners."

"Or wives," giggled Clara. "We shall have a competition, I think, to see who shall have the most suitors. What do you say?"

Poor Clara with her rabbit teeth and constant squint, the hay-like patch of yellow on her scalp, and her spotted face! Her charm and humor were commendable, but when did young men ever seek a lady out for those? Clara waited, nodding her head up and down, her giggles sounding like squeaks from an unlatched gate in the wind.

"You will have the advantage, Mistress Clara, as you know all the gentlemen hereabouts," I said.

"Still, we shall have such sport!"

❧❦❧

"I WON'T GO," I said to Mother Winifred when we were locking up for the night.

"Ah," was her objection, and I knew there would be more. We were upstairs in her kitchen when she spoke again. "That is a wise decision, for I am certain His Excellency Thorne has devised this ball to find you, Princess Eleanor."

"How good to know my father's cohort of spies stretches the length of Rosemyre and has remained loyal to him."

"Nothing by chance, my lady. Even this ball. It may even be an opportunity for you to secure the King and Queen's release."

My mind was changing by the time Ralph returned from whatever he did during the day. I found him in the small sitting room with a cup of mead, his stockinged feet pointed at a fire.

"It's a cold night," I greeted, pulling my

shawl closer.

He rose, smiling, and gestured to the bench. "Join me, Lady."

"The snows will come soon; they always do right before Christmas," I said, it being the first thought that came to me.

"Another season to miss your parents' company and the safety of Rosemyre Castle," he said, glancing at me.

"Yes."

The fire crackled, and flames danced and wavered. I could have sworn I saw the image of the Angel and Rose in the yellows, oranges, and reds. We sat in silence. I was glad of his presence though I couldn't tell whether he was glad of mine or the duty to which he was beholden.

So many people were pledged to my father on behalf of my safekeeping. If ever my father regained his kingdom, I would ask a boon to repay my guardians threefold, even if I had to sell one of my dower castles to do it.

"This Christmas Revels," I ventured now, looking over at Ralph. He was frowning. Just as I expected. "It is a masked ball, is it not?"

"Yes, my lady."

"Dressed and disguised, I could attend."

"It would be too dangerous!"

"Ralph, I would know my enemy and the enemy of my people. I could slip in and slip out. No one would notice, not with all of Flowergate to the Sapphire Hills crowding the ballroom," I argued. "He doesn't know what I look like. It's been four years since The War began. I was a skinny little girl when they brought me here. No one has really seen me, have they?"

"No . . ."

"They'd see a young lady of a fine house in a fine gown and mask. And I'm certain I would not be the only young lady attending."

Ralph's sigh was his disapproval, but by morning I'd devised what I thought was the cleverest of plans and waited for him in the passageway to the main door.

"Lady Ella!" he greeted, surprised to find me there.

"Good morning, Ralph. I trust you slept well?"

"I do—I did."

"What I remember of Godrick Thorne is that he thinks only of his own gain, and his lies are truths to him. He loves flattery."

"That's the right of it, Lady. Though where you heard this,"

"Come with me!"

We went to my chapel, and as we entered, I pointed to the Great Book sitting atop the prayer desk.

"I was old enough to attend royal audiences at Court, but this will confirm my memory." Saying this, I turned to a page in the Great Book and pointed to my mother's wobbly handwriting, which verified my statement.

Ralph studied the entry in the Great Book, and then looked at it again, then turned a page, and another. Finally, he nodded.

"A young lady might tease and flatter upon this evening if only to learn secrets. What do you say?"

"I'm sure Mother Winifred and you will outdo yourselves to make a gown and disguise."

"And will you escort me, Ralph? You could come as my guardian angel."

"In golden armor, my lady."

Chapter 9

W E WERE AT work on my gown and disguise for the masked ball the moment Mother Winifred and I returned from hearing mass the next morning, and we'd broken our fast. Again, Ralph disappeared to do whatever it was he did, and I barely noticed he was gone until the sun was setting. Mother Winifred said that it was time for Vespers before I could ask about Ralph. Our work was draped with linen sheets to protect it from dust and damp, the tools put away in their cupboards, and missals and shawls fetched.

The town was pretty during the day, but at sunset, it was breathtaking, with vines and plants everywhere tinged with daylight's last gold. It was winter, and it would be some weeks before I could see them blooming, however. It was my fervent prayer every night that I would not stay long to see the first spring blossoms in this little paradise but be reunited with my parents, even if it meant going alone to Bramble Court in the Greylands. This was my prayer as I knelt in the church and inhaled the sweetness of the frankincense and fixed my eyes on the gentle face of the Redeemer gazing at me from His cross behind the altar.

As I rose and turned to leave, I noticed a young gentleman dozing at the back of the church. He leaned against one of the wooden posts that divided the nave into three sections and looked familiar because he was the young man from Mistress Temby's shop in Flowergate.

The owner of the garter royal!

"Excuse me," I greeted him. He started snoring. "Excuse me! Sir! I say, are you well?"

"Wha-?" he yawned after he snorted a bit and woke up.

"Sir, are you well? You've been asleep," I said.

"It's the sermons," he yawned again, and then he recognized me. "I know you! You're the Shop Girl of Flowergate! Do you have my garter?"

"Shh!" I scolded.

He took a step towards the sacristy, put a finger to his lips, and motioned for me to follow.

"Who do you think I am? I'm no tavern girl for assignations!"

"Well, who do you think I am, Mistress?" he scoffed in return, adding, "It's not only your reputation to be considered!"

We might have stood there all night arguing over one another's virtue but for Mother Winifred's intervention. It seemed I wasn't the only one who recognized the gentleman, for she curtseyed before him and said, "Pardon, Your Grace," and dragged me out of the church.

"I would like to know why you did that!" I complained as we hurried quicker than usual back to the shop. "I have a garter of his that wants mending. I was given a commission to finish it by his twenty-first—"

"Will you be silent, Princess!" Mother Winifred hissed.

"I will not!" I snapped.

"Not another word, mind!"

As soon as we were in the living

quarters of the shop and the doors were barred, she started pacing and muttering, "After all we've done, that this should happen! We must make certain he stays silent! Ralph will know what to do; he always knows what is right and good. By the angels and saints, we have to finish what is started!" She turned on me. "I'm afraid the Christmas Revels are now out of the question, my dear. It won't be safe. Not with the prince in Sneaton and Ruswarp. Who knows where his allegiance lies?"

"Couldn't he be one of my father's men?" I spoke up meekly. "There are enough of them lurking about. Besides, I am the Princess—"

"It would be too dangerous. Not only for you but your parents."

"I think not!"

"Not. Another. WORD!"

And with that, I stood on the other side of my chamber door as the bolt was thrown and the key turned in the lock.

I thumped on the door and stamped my foot.

"YOU'LL HAVE TO let me out eventually!"

I shouted at Ralph several hours later.

"It's for your own good, Eleanor."

"Ah, so now you call me by my true name! If I am Princess Eleanor, you will do as you're told and now! And you will do well to obey!"

"I answer to your lord and king, your grace."

"I don't see him here. Let me out!"

"In time, Princess."

I thumped on the door and stamped my foot.

This played out for several days.

Meals were brought, bathing tub, fresh clothes and underthings, an occasional book, and my needlework were carried in by servants and sometimes by Ralph or Mother Winifred, but the key was always turned and the bolt thrown once they were gone. I tried to slip under one or the other's arm to no avail, for the other was always waiting in the passageway. I had more freedom in the tower at Flowergate!

One morning I woke and found my revels gown and disguise on a wicker form standing in the center of the room. A basket of sewing notions sat on a table. Sensing that a change of plan was afoot, I whiled away my hours of captivity sewing this magical thing I'd dreamed up and finished on the afternoon of the Christmas Revels.

My plan was to be a flower faery, complete with wings of shimmering silk, that would be decorated with embroidered roses and flowers to match those on the soft silk fabric of my gown. The shift of purest lawn in a saffron shade and the over-gown of dark blue velvet were decorated with gold and silver vines and leaves. The mask was like one found in Venice—painted stiffened fabric decorated with gems and silk flowers. Now they were draped on the wicker form for only me to admire, for judging from the noise and laughter downstairs, I would not be attending the ball. Sure enough, the door below slammed shut, and I heard the key in the lock. The carriage wheels on the cobblestones confirmed my solitary state.

I climbed into bed and watched the shadows of tree branches and leaves, of fireflies, as I said my prayers and drifted off to sleep.

The clock striking midnight woke me for some reason; usually it made no difference. As I sat up yawning and rubbing my eyes, I noticed the shadow of a woman beside the window. Reaching for the candle, I waved the flame towards her.

"Ariella?!" I exclaimed. "What are you doing here? How did you get in?"

"A flower faery, your grace?" said Ariella coming into the light. "That's a bit obvious, don't you think? Even a man as dense in thought as Godrick Thorne would figure it out." She lit the lamps in the room by gesturing at them, and standing before me wasn't the sulky, jealous seamstress from Mistress Temby's shop but a faery. The aura surrounding her was pale lavender, and she was silver, except for her lips and cheeks, which were pink with color. Ariella turned to study the gown and its trappings.

"Don't you think it's lovely?" I asked, crawling off the bed. "Mistress Winifred brought it in to make me happy, I suppose. Though where I shall wear it, I don't know."

"Do you think Winifred did you the kindness?"

"Why wouldn't she?"

"Think again, Princess." She turned to

the dress and walked around the wicker form, inspecting my work. "Well, it will have to do," she sighed. "Aha! I know what!"

A wig of russet curls shot with gold and scattered with dewdrops of diamonds of sapphires stood on a wooden form that appeared on the table.

Ariella smiled at me, and at her invitation, I inspected the wig and other magical treasures that started to appear where she pointed: A pair of azure slippers and a cape of shimmering gold. Both were embroidered with pink and silver stars that twinkled.

"Get dressed and hurry now," she said in a kindly voice.

I hadn't removed my bed robe and shift, but there I stood in the gown, over-gown, cape, and slippers, the mask on my face, the wig on top of my hair.

"Surely this is not the Shop Girl of Flowergate," I whispered, peering into a looking glass.

"Surely not. Take my hand,"

As soon as my fingers entwined in hers, I felt as light as a feather, as if I was floating in a dream. Nothing made any sense, and the colors that swirled around me were soothing and exciting at the same time. I suddenly felt sleepy and nodded off, but when I woke, I was on the top of the grand staircase in the Guild Hall in Sneaton and Ruswarp, and the first lavish entertainment of the Christmas Revels, the Grand Masked Ball, was before me with all of its glorious color and wealth.

Chapter 10

I KNEW WHAT to do even before Ariella offered instruction. She handed me a scroll bound with a scarlet ribbon: my pedigree. A page came up, bowed, ex-tended his arm, and I took it, passing off the scroll to an usher who unfurled the parchment and called, "Lady Sapphira, Duchess of Azurene in The Sapphire Hills!"

A few gentlemen offered me a cursory glance, a complimentary smile, but other than that, I was one more guest to crowd the ballroom. After my introduction, no one gave me a single glance as I descended the stairs, kicking out the hems and with each dainty step until I was standing on the perimeter of dancing couples in the charming ballroom. I was offered a cup of mead by a porter and took it gratefully, for my mouth was dry from nerves. If I had to speak, I'm sure I would have brayed like a donkey or croaked like a frog.

I moved slowly through the crowd towards the plinth where Godrick Thorne sat with his consort Tamsine and his sons, Roderick, Warwick, and Wulfrick. They resembled their surname, Thorne: all were thin, reedy, colorless, and prickly. The last I guessed because they each, in turn, refused to acknowledge anyone who approached to offer their greetings for the Holy Season of Christmas.

What would happen if I approached?

Just as I was steps away from them, a gentleman took my hand and, kissing it, said, "That would be a grievous error, Princess Eleanor, trust me."

It was the Somnambulant Prince who caught my attention.

He bowed and winked at me from behind his fox mask. Before I could protest or make up a clever lie to send him off my scent, he whispered, "There are many in this room who know the Princess Eleanor of Rosemyre," he said as he led me in a dance that was starting up, clearly to steer me away from the Thornes. Now he pointed towards Ralph Falconer, dressed as my guardian angel with his golden armor and splendid multi-colored wings; next, to

Ariella, who still glowed with a sometimes silver, sometimes lavender aura; then to Mother Winifred, who looked like a saint in her many robes and halo. He gestured towards Harold, the knight from Flowergate dressed as a priest, to Eaelfred, the wise schoolmaster, and Mistress Temby, a milkmaid of all things. And Master Moorehead was wearing the most colorful and incredible pair of stockings, and not a hole in them. The Prince showed me others in the room, from cat to dragon by their disguises, as we spun and whirled about. "We would willingly give our lives for the heiress of Rosemyre, The Greenhavens, and Keeper of The Sapphire Hills," he whispered as we danced. "We would follow you to Bramble Court in the Greylands."

I swallowed the lump growing in my throat and was glad he couldn't see my happy tears. Princesses of the great legends had but one champion. I had several.

We spun about and changed partners several times now, and mine were predictably Ralph, Harold, and Eaelfred. When the dance ended, I was ready to thank the Prince when I looked up and saw Godrick Thorne smiling down at me.

"We've not had the pleasure of an introduction, Lady," he greeted in a voice that was like his reedy, colorless, frame and bland clothing. He looked down his nose at me, for it was long, sharp, and was pointed directly at my face. His eyes, were they not rheumy and bloodshot, might be his best feature, for they were dark brown in color and perfectly round like an owl's.

When I opened my mouth to speak, Ralph said, "You will forgive Lady Sapphira—her lady-in-waiting says the lady has been ill and has lost her voice." Clever Ralph! I nodded demurely and didn't bother to look at Thorne when he lifted my chin with a cold, boney finger. Thorne studied me, frowning at first and then smiling and nodding. Finally, his lips touched my hand and lingered while he looked up at me. Everyone around us whispered and watched.

"Hah!" a gentleman nearby laughed. "Excellency Thorne has found his new concubine!"

I shuddered. Was that my fate? From

the look on Tamsine's chalk-white face, it would seem so.

"You and I shall dance," Thorne announced and snapped his fingers. People moved away and made a circle around us as a pavane was struck, and we stepped silently to the stately measures. Whenever I could, I looked for Ralph. Fortunately, he was never out of my sight. It was the most prolonged and most tiresome dance I could remember. At the final notes, I dropped in a curtesy, my gown and over-gown rippling around me in iridescent blue waves tinged with gold. I must have been a remarkable sight, for there were murmurs of approval from both women and men, like those when my mother would enter the Audience Court. Thorne studied me as I looked up at him, and then he nodded and walked away, saying, "Adequate. She will do."

Ralph was there to help me up, fortunately, for I seemed to be glued to the floor and was sure to fall over if I tried to stand alone.

"I want to go," I whispered.

"Not yet," Ralph said, and his eyes slid to his right where the Somnambulant

Prince stood. "This is your truest friend."
Saying this, Ralph handed me off to the
Prince for a dance. It was a basse danse,
courtly and slow, with very little
movement, which gave us time to
converse in whispers and take the measure
of one another.

"You know my name, but I have yet to
learn yours," I said as we passed by,
touching palms.

"Athelstan," he answered with a yawn.

"And your home is where?"

"I am a vassal to Rosemyre. My lands
are in The Greenhavens at Worthy."

"Well met, Athelstan of Worthy."

"And you, my Lady Sapphira."

Our dance was pleasant, and for once I
didn't feel clumsy or as if I would topple
over. We kept each other company until
the Master of Ceremonies rapped his staff
on the floor and said the festivities were
over. I looked to the plinth and saw that
Thorne and his sons and consort were
gone. Mother Winifred and Ralph were at
my side and gently leading me through the
crowd to the door. I looked back at
Athelstan, and he smiled and blew a kiss.
I felt a happy chill and nodded in return,

looking back again, and delighted that he still watched.

Chapter 11

"LADY SAPPHIRA OF Azurene in The Sapphire Hills is all anyone can talk of in the market square!" Mother Winifred crowed when she returned from her shopping the next day.

I looked up from my mending of Athelstan's garter royal and smiled. I didn't care so much that I had caused gossip but wanted to see the Prince again. I laughed softly, and Mother Winifred patted my cheek.

"You did well, my lady! You have every right to laugh."

"I was wondering when I might see Prince Athelstan of Worthy again."

"Ah! You needn't worry about that, Princess," Mother Winifred said. "I expect that will be tonight. Excellency Thorne has called for another ball! He was taken by a certain lady." Here she put a finger to her lips and winked as if to share a secret.

"Taken?" I asked, fearful of what that meant, even though I knew the answer.

"Oh yes, he has a fancy to find a new consort. And this would give you a fine opportunity to ruin his ambitions. When you are his consort, you may demand the release of your parents—"

I leapt to my feet and flew at her, fists clenched. "How can you say that! I will not be anyone's consort, not until my parents are released from The Greylands, and even then, I will heed my Mother's counsel! For shame! Here I thought you were one of my Father's counselors!"

"My, my!" Mother Winifred exclaimed, taking me by the shoulders. "A princess knows to keep her temper and her thoughts to herself."

"Do you not know? Can you not guess?" and after saying this, I fled to the solitude of my chambers at the top of the house.

How could I betray my family and kingdom by making an alliance with Godrick Thorne? All marriages were for political and economic reasons, and I knew mine would be no different.

"But Thorne?" I demanded of Ralph

when he visited that evening at twilight.

"Why do you think Thorne? There were hundreds of ladies at the ball. You have a high opinion of yourself, Princess Eleanor."

His comment stung, and I sulked over it while I dressed for the ball and rode in the carriage with Ralph and Mother Winifred. Only when I saw Athelstan standing in a group of young men did my spirits rise. He excused himself from their company and greeted me with a kiss on my palm and one of his delicious glances, the blue of his eyes sparkling through his mask and the smile capturing my heart.

For most of the evening, we danced and dined together. I paused to join Ralph and Mother Winifred every now and then as it would have been improper to let Athelstan take all my attention.

I wouldn't have objected if he had.

Athelstan was nodding towards the garden and I would have joined him there if only to kiss that wonderful mouth had it not been for the Master of Ceremonies thumping his staff on the floor. The room was silent, and we all looked to the plinth where Godrick Thorne and his sons and consort stood. Another minute passed, and Thorne slowly stepped down and walked towards me, the crowd parting as he did so, of course. Ralph was at my side then, taking my hand as I tried a curtsey. Thorne glared at him and snapped his fingers at me.

"Lady Sapphira, all of Rosemyre is enchanted with you. May we see the real beauty behind this mask?"

I made ready to speak but then paused and felt Ralph's reassuring squeeze of my hand as he said to Thorne, "Is it not the custom of the Christmas Revels to stay masked until the Eve of the Nativity? I'm sure the lady would not wish to break with tradition."

"Her grace and wit, her apparent beauty, demands it," Thorne said darkly. And then, "I demand it."

"Why spoil the Revels with curiosity?" Ralph asked. He pulled me gently towards the staircase, and Athelstan pushed through the crowd to join us. We were nearly free when Thorne grabbed my shoulder and pulled me around, tearing the mask from my face.

"I will have satisfaction, Princess

Eleanor of Rosemyre!"

Gasps, whispers, and the rustle of fabric, the clink of swords and spurs as people knelt filled the uncomfortable void while Thorne and I stared at one another.

"Get up! Damn you all, get up! She is not your sovereign; she is my prisoner!" Thorne shouted at everyone. They took their time moving, which angered him even more. "Her parents are traitors and have relinquished their titles and crowns! *She* is a traitor!"

Ralph and Athelstan had their hands on sword pommels as Thorne's knights approached on his command, and a few parries and thrusts were exchanged until Tamsine wailed, "I beg of you! Stop this! Let her go!"

Athelstan was intent on proving my champion until one of Thorne's knights put a knife to his throat.

"Athelstan! No!" I screamed. That ended the fracas before it led to injury or death.

"Take her away," Thorne growled.

"No!!!" shouted Athelstan.

Athelstan's look was of anguish as I was led off, his arms pinioned by Thorne's men and the sword taken from him; I turned for a last look and saw his body slumped over as he lost consciousness. I realized all was lost and fainted as any proper princess would under the circumstance.

∽⧉∼

I WAS HELD in apartments in the Guild-hall with two knights to guard the door. Upon waking, I found Lady Tamsine and Thorne's son Roderick sitting on either side of the bed, reading books.

"Ah, so you're awake!" Tamsine pronounced, slamming her book shut.

Her movements startled Roderick, who alternately frowned and stared at me.

"She's not much to worry about, is she?" Roderick sniffed.

"She is the heiress to Rosemyre, The Greenhavens, and Keeper of The Sapphire Hills," said Tamsine sharply as she fanned me with her book. "She is something."

"Would you please stop that?" I asked, batting away the book.

"You look feverish. Perhaps you should change out of that heavy velvet. Roderick, you will leave while the Princess disrobes and puts on something more

suitable for her caging," Tamsine instructed.

"I will not! She's to be my bride, so I
might as well have a look at what Father's
bought me," Roderick said, winking at me.

"I thought I wasn't much to worry
about," I snapped.

"True, but you're uncommonly pretty.
Now come then, Princess. I want to see
what is mine—all of it."

"You will not! Get out! Both of you!"
I demanded, sitting up. I grabbed Tamsine's book and hurled it at Roderick, the
spine striking him smack-dab in the eye.

"Ow! You little witch! That wasn't
necessary!" he whined and, covering his
eye, fled from the room.

Tamsine raised a hand to strike me, and
I flinched, ready to accept punishment
when she lowered her hand and smoothed
back her hair.

"It's not your fault what's happened,
and that's the first time anyone has
touched the spoiled brat. I say good for
you, Princess!"

"You're his spy!" I hissed.

"No, never his," she answered before
leaving.

While I pondered her meaning, the fact the door had not been locked behind Lady Tamsine escaped me while I searched the bedchamber for something to use as a weapon in case Thorne or his son came to visit. It was the room of a prosperous merchant with nice cupboards, chests, and benches of polished oak and whitewashed timbered walls. The pretty hangings around the bed were made of flower-embroidered silk. I would have dismissed them as a typical decoration for a lady's bower but for the words embroidered on the hems:

God Give Blessing and Honor to
Those Who Serve the True King.

Then I saw what was surely meant for me. Draped over one of the chests were a simple dress, cloak, and hood, all in a plum colorway. There were riding boots and a leather satchel on the floor next to the chest. I peeked inside and found a flask, some bread, cheese, and dried meat.

And a small, elegant sword precisely the right size for someone of my stature.

Chapter 12

F TAMSINE WANTED me to escape, I'd not disappoint her. Once out of my ball gown and in the simple travel clothes, I peeked out a window and saw that dawn was fast approaching. No one was about on the street below. Even the market square was empty, save a meandering cat that decided to perch itself on an open stall counter. Now was the perfect time to leave.

The bedchamber door opened smoothly without ghastly squeaks or moans, and the boards beneath my boots did not creak as I tip-toed down the stairs. A servant leaning against the wall snored and sputtered. A maid seemed to have fallen asleep in the kitchen where she was doing the washing up. Curious, I crept through rooms in the guildhall and found people sleeping in the most unimaginable of states; there were cooks in the middle of kneading bread dough; liveried servants nodding over trays of sweetmeats and mead. Sentries leaned on their pikes and snored where they stood.

What sort of a place was this?

I knew some people practiced the dark arts of magic and knew there were those whose magic was for good. Perhaps this was one of those times?

I was confident even the guildhall was asleep, for the stones and planks were silent as I looked about.

Toward the back of the kitchen, I found a pantry and tried the door, and peeking in, I saw Athelstan trussed up like a goose. He was also asleep. No one was about, so I untied him and shook him.

"Athelstan? My prince? Are you well? Sir! Please wake up! We must leave this place. Godrick Thorne wants to marry me to one of his sons or take me for himself! Please!"

I sat back on my knees, exasperated, and looked around the barrels of grain, the shelves of jars and packages. I didn't know which one pepper was, for certainly a bit of that up the nose would make him sneeze.

He was so beautiful, snoring and

sighing in his sleep, his hair falling over his brow and into his closed eyes. I couldn't help myself as I brushed his hair away and kissed first his brow and then his lips—our first kiss.

Athelstan woke then, eyes opening slowly, and then a smile crossed his lips. He reached up to bring my face closer and we kissed again. And again.

Outside the pantry, I heard yawns and coughs, some exclamations of 'Not again!'

"We'd better leave," said Athelstan as he shoved himself to his feet and taking my hand, led the way out of the pantry and kitchen to the courtyard.

"Thank you for rescuing me," I said as we hurried along.

"It was you who saved me. Now I'll be able to sleep like any man, and hopefully that won't be until our work is done. First, I must take you to Mistress Winifred's house."

"Thorne will go there first."

"Then we must take another course. Ralph thought as much. I think—yes! I have a map he sketched. Come,"

"Ralph?" I demanded. "Where is he?"

"Waiting in the Forest of Briar," said

Athelstan matter-of-factly.

"Why is he there and not with us? He left me to the mercy of Thorne!" I grumbled.

"I hardly think so, Princess."

"And where is Mother Winifred? Harold? Have they deserted me?"

"Why would you think that?" Athelstan laughed.

"Because they're not here!"

"I forgot that you've never been in the real world. Always kept in a castle and then the tower at Flowergate. My apologies, Princess. We should have explained all."

I stopped and crossed my arms over my breasts and glared at him.

"Come, we have to go. And quickly, too."

"Not until you tell me what's happening and why."

"Ralph Falconer is waiting in the Forest of Briar with an army. Mother Winifred, Master Moorehead, Ariella, Lady Tode, oh, and the strange lady from Flowergate."

"Mistress Temby?"

"Yes, she. The gossip. She almost ruined our plans. You see, we are going to rescue the true King and Queen. Your prayers are answered, Princess. Ralph and Mother Winifred knew you couldn't have done it on your own,"

"Given half a chance..."

"I don't doubt that for a moment. We can talk when we get into the forest. If we stand here a moment longer, those Thorne knights coming our way will capture us." Athelstan grabbed my arm and pulled me along as I looked back and saw knights running from the guildhall in pursuit.

At the end of the market square were horses tethered outside an alehouse. "Can you ride?" he demanded as he took two enormous horses.

"No,"

Within seconds I was lifted onto a saddle, and I was riding for my life, following Athelstan out of Sneaton and Ruswarp.

Chapter 13

WE DIDN'T STOP until we were well away from town, the Caves of Wormhill like pockmarks on the northern lands, and the great northwestern forests started to loom before us. It was going on noon, by the position of the pale winter sun above us, Athelstan said, and we stopped at a stream to rest the horses. There were some felled oaks and sycamore that made a moss-covered hideaway and no sooner had Athelstan dismounted than he lifted the saddlebag from his horse and brought it over, dropping it well within the confines of the tree trunks. He walked the horse to the stream and then turned to me, frowning. I was still in the saddle.

"We must stop to rest, Princess," he said.

"I'm fine where I am," I replied. To say the truth, I was too ashamed that I didn't know if I could dismount without hurting myself or the horse. My legs and bottom were in agony from the pace we'd traveled. If I'd never been a horsewoman before, I was now. I guessed my legs would have a trail of blisters and my bottom...

Athelstan sighed and gently lifted me off the saddle. I winced and tried not to cry out in pain. Once on the ground, I hobbled to our campsite.

"You'll be fine in another day," he reassured me, tapping me on the nose, the only place I didn't hurt.

"How far to the Forest of Briar?"

"Another day or two, if it doesn't snow— three, then."

"We will be at Bramble Court in the Greylands by Christmas."

"Do you think so?"

I shrugged. "I don't know. It just came to me."

Athelstan patted the blanket he'd spread on the ground, and I slowly, painfully, eased myself down, squeaking just a little as I sat. He chuckled, and I laughed with him.

"Soon you shall be with your parents and once more the heiress to Rosemyre, The Greenhavens, and Keeper of The

Sapphire Hills."

"I have indeed prayed for this day to come," I admitted, and then, glancing at him, "And where will you be, Athelstan of Worthy?"

"With my mother in our castle. She will be consulting a great list of brides for me, and I shall be—sleeping. I hope. That will delay the inevitable."

Without thinking, I said, "Were I on that list, would you sleep?"

He responded with a kiss and then leaned his head next to mine. We sat thus for a long while. I soon heard him snore and breathing deeply. The horses were grazing by the stream, and winter birds foraging in the brown grass and bracken. I noticed the owls on a sycamore branch and thought it odd for my lessons told me owls were night creatures. However, I felt comforted by their presence and started to feel weary, barely able to keep my eyes open. This must be a good sleep, I thought, and found myself nodding off.

❧☙

ATHELSTAN GENTLY SHOOK ME and whispered things like 'love' and 'sweet-heart' as I woke from a peaceful sleep. I opened my eyes to his handsome face and beautiful smile blocking out the sun, which was lower in the sky than when we first stopped to rest.

"Thorne's men are almost upon us. I saw their banners about two miles away," Athelstan said, and despite the pain and fatigue, I mounted and we were riding north again and this time with rain and sleet lashing at our faces. As much as I hated the burning and stinging of ice, I was glad it slowed our progress, for it made riding more comfortable. Mother Earth was certainly favoring us, for the sleet and rain stopped, the clouds disappeared, and a clear sky was above us so that we could continue to travel well into the night; the snow-dusted paths glowed from the moonlight and showed us the way to the Forest of Briar.

We were greeted by campfires and torches outside tents and their orange and amber reflection on swords and spears once we rode out of the vale. A large pavilion was set back from smaller tents crowded together at the south end of the clearing, and it was to this we rode. I heard the whispers of "Princess Eleanor!"

and "Hail Lamb of God, Angel and Rose!" as we passed soldiers. I acknowledged their salutes and bows in the manner of my mother the Queen: with polite nods and making eye contact, sometimes offering smiles.

Once more, Athelstan helped me down. I ambled towards the pavilion, making sure my back was straight, and I showed no sign of pain. A lady of royal blood does not show her weakness to those who depend on her. My mother had said that to me more than once when I moaned over a scraped knee or a fingertip bruised by the point of an embroidery needle.

Two guards parted the flaps so that I could enter an enclosure that was as magnificent as an audience court.

How was it possible to have a polished pearl floor and a silver throne decorated with mosaics of roses made from opals? The tent poles were made of silver, too, but vines of gold wound round them, and in place of flowers were precious jewels: rubies, sapphires, emeralds, diamonds, and topazes. The hangings were thick velvet embroidered with my device, the angel holding a rose in silver and gold thread.

Behind one of the hangings was a bed, as rich and luxurious as my surroundings: fat pillows stuffed with down with silk cases and fur-trimmed coverlets of velvet. Standing amid this opulence was Ralph Falconer and two other men who bowed as I came forward.

"My lords, I have kept my promise. I give you Princess Eleanor," Athelstan said as he brought me forward and bade me sit on the throne. The three men knelt, and it was then I saw the wings—great spans like eagles' and each tipped in gold, silver, and amethyst color at the ends.

"What is this mask, sirs?" I questioned. "Shall we have dancing and feasting for the Lord's Nativity here in this wilderness?"

"No, Princess," said Ralph smiling up at me. "You prayed for the safe return of your parents' to their kingdom, and we have come to assist you. I am Raphael, and my companions are Michael and Gabriel. We will ride with you to Bramble Court, and you will take back your father's kingdom from Godrick Thorne of the Greylands."

I stood involuntarily, ignoring the pain,

and stared, trembling, at the archangels who still knelt before me. Athelstan had joined them, and thus they waited.

When I finally found my voice, I whispered. "Then it is true that with God nothing is impossible. This is the Lord's doing, and it is marvelous in our eyes."

I stepped down and with a gesture, bade my celestial knights-errant and prince rise. They did so as one and I was dwarfed by their height and magnificence. Even Athelstan took on new stature. He now turned and gestured to pages that were standing apart from us: Olivia and Oliver. They brought a crown and orb, which I accepted as they backed away, but not before smiling.

"This is not our kingdom," I said with a bold voice. "It is that of our father, Humphrey, the twenty-third of that name and King of Rosemyre. I take these in his absence," and here I raised the orb and the sword given to me by Raphael, "and swear to you that I will not fail his people and will make good his name again."

A cheer went up, and the tent seemed to quake as the men around me shouted, "Rosemyre! Rosemyre!"

"With your leave, we will ride in the morning. I pray you lead us," said Michael, looking to me and then his companions.

"With joy!" I said tearfully.

Chapter 14

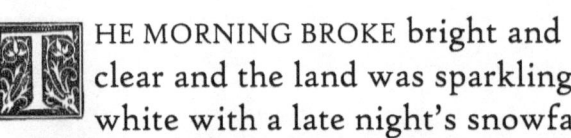HE MORNING BROKE bright and clear and the land was sparkling white with a late night's snowfall. Campfires were sending up the delicious aromas of soups and vegetable pies, and there was also the tang of frankincense. While I dressed behind the bedcurtains, I could hear men arming themselves and talking about the battle to come. Some laughed, and others spoke of fear; some whispered prayers.

"Good morrow, Princess," Athelstan greeted when I emerged dressed in my riding clothes, boots, and hooded cloak. I gasped, for he was dressed in armor and looked like a romantic figure to me. He stepped forward and kissed my palm in greeting.

"Good morning, Athelstan. Pray God, you're not fighting, are you?" I asked.

"Of course I am, Lady. I am sworn to Rosemyre. Gladly, I might add."

"I, I would die if you were to fall in battle," I stammered. "Never again being able to talk with you, or ride, or dance,"

"Then I will have to be sure to stay on my horse," Athelstan teased. We embraced awkwardly, and he lifted my chin for a kiss. "I know we'll win if I have your favor with me."

A knight at a tournament rode into the lists with his lady's favor tied on his arm or lance. I had no length of ribbon or lace, but I did have the garter royal. Its repair was unfinished, but the motto was legible. I slipped out of his arms and found my satchel, taking from it the garter.

"Will this do?" I asked. I knelt and tied it around his right leg just under the knee.

"I'll return it to you after we've rescued the King and Queen." He kissed my forehead. "This I promise, Eleanor."

I said nothing; how could I say that I wanted him to return more than anything and that I loved him? Would he think me foolish, or worse, laugh? I might have said what I was thinking, but for the sounding of trumpets. The sound was melodious, soothing, the most unwarlike call I'd ever heard.

"It's time," Athelstan said quietly. I heard the fear in his voice and said nothing in an effort to quell my own. Taking my hand, he led me outside.

No one, not even my father, could have been prepared for what greeted us.

Several hundred of Athelstan's fyrd called up from Worthy were assembling in battle formation—footmen, huscarls, and cavalry.

The Worthy banner was everywhere: the golden chalice on an azure ground encircled by grapevines. They made up the vanguard. The center and left and right flanks were a vast army of angels.

Angels.

Michael, of course, led the center. His angels glowed with a golden, soft light. Raphael, my Ralph, led the left flank and his angels were silver. Gabriel had the right flank of angels that were pale purple and glowed with the brilliance of amethysts. They rode magnificent white steeds barded in their colors. The device was all the same. A cross like that found in ancient hoards dug up on the eastern shores of my father's kingdom—round and with a garnet at its intersection—was embroidered on plain yellow cloth.

Athelstan let go of my hand and saddled up. His eyes were fixed on the horizon before him and he was alert. I'd never seen him so preoccupied in the short time we'd been acquainted.

"My lady, we must ride."

I turned, surprised by Ariella's voice, and saw that she wore armor and was radiant with a pale light. To be in this mysterious yet Godly cohort gave me courage.

Olivia and Oliver were at my side now. I knelt to see their solemn faces. "You must stay here. We'll come for you when all is done."

"We'll dance at your wedding," Olivia said.

Why did the children come to me, I wondered, and reading my thoughts, Ariella said, "A test of selflessness is often rewarded."

Kisses and hugs were exchanged when a groom brought forward a chestnut stallion and with his help I mounted the saddle. No sooner had I done this than celestial huscarls, two from each of the battles, formed a guard around me.

The trumpets sounded their music again, and silently the Archangels rode forward. Master Moorehead sidled up next to me, carrying my banner of the Angel with the Glowing Rose.

We began our ride out of the Forest of Briar north to Bramble Court.

❦

WE FLEW LIKE the wind. By the end of the week we were at the boundaries of The Greylands and the massive pile of rocks that was a castle called Bramble Court. Its defense was an enclosure of bracken that was ten feet high. The thorns on the branches, Athelstan said, were as sharp as swords and warned me not to go near, as I would see the bones and decaying remains of many knights who died trying to rescue The King and Queen of Rosemyre.

"Our attempt will not be so dangerous, not with an army of angels," I replied.

"I had a demon to fight once," Saint Michael spoke up as he reined in beside us.

"You prevailed. So shall we," I said.

"By your faith," he answered and bowed his head, a hand against his heart.

The armies now ranged themselves in battles as we approached. Saint Raphael held me back as Athelstan and his fyrd lined up behind Saint Michael's vanguard.

"You will wait here until it is time," he said.

How I wanted to ride with Athelstan and the knights of Rosemyre! That thought was now obsession as trumpets sounded and were answered by those of Thorne's army now marching through the bracken gates. I kicked the spurs into the chestnut's flanks; it responded by trotting first and then at a gallop. I knew instinctively to move with the horse yet stay low in the saddle to keep my seat. I had almost caught up with the fyrd when Ariella rode up and blocked my path. The chestnut reared, but I did not fall.

"You will not go further, Lady!" she warned. "Now is not the time."

The battle began, not with two front lines clashing and swords meeting, but with trumpets announcing the warrior angels as they rode through Thorne's army and parted it like the Red Sea. Foot soldiers and knights perished under the angels' swords. A path was cleared for Athelstan and his fyrd and they advanced at great speed with weapons drawn, ready to overtake any of Thorne's men still standing or horsed. I could see my prince in the thick of the fighting. His armor was bright and unmistakable, like a beacon to the enemy. Fortunately, Gabriel's men formed a shield around him and held off Thorne's knights as Worthy's fyrd kept advancing towards the castle. Hand to hand and mounted combat were inevitable and I kept my sight on Athelstan, watching and praying that the blood spraying around him wasn't his.

The fyrd reached the castle and now attacked the bracken like dead wood in a forest or garden. But this was no ordinary plant. Athelstan took heavy losses as the fyrd was repelled by the deadly thorns. The screams were terrifying as men died on the bracken as surely as if run through with swords. Still, Athelstan shouted at his men to regroup and they made a shield wall as in olden days. Marching in one great line, the fyrd cut and chopped at the bracken as it advanced: spears, swords, and seaxes stabbed and slashed, then shields went up as the bracken, like snakes, writhed, flailed, and attacked. It was the right tactic for the bracken was cut down and the entrance to the castle was visible.

Ariella unsheathed a magnificent wand capped by a sapphire encircled by crystals that glowed with different colors. She turned to me and smiled, saying, "Now, Princess! Now is the time!"

Kicking the horse gently with my heels, I followed her and with our angelic huscarls, we followed the path made by the angels and the fyrd.

The bracken was frightening to behold. I could have sworn I saw dead eyes and pale faces within the shadows of intertwined branches and trunks. Some of the branches reared back and struck out at us. I found my small sword and took swipes at them, hitting my mark occasionally, and was cheered on by Ariella.

We followed the fyrd through the gatehouse. Our angel cohort guarded us as we rode into the great bailey. Household buildings, the baking house, and breweries, the smiths and chapel, were empty as we thundered in.

"Dismount and surround the perimeter! Swords at the ready!" Athelstan shouted to his men.

I followed his instructions and waited

with Ariella as the fyrd formed more
shield walls in the bailey and Athelstan's
elite guard, the huscarls, took up formation
around him, joined by the Archangels.
Athelstan gave the signal and they went
up the stairs into the donjon. I slipped
away and followed them. Before Ariella
knew I was gone it was too late for her to
do anything.

Chapter 15

EVERYTHING AROUND US was covered with or being encroached upon by branches covered with thorns. Burning lamps hung from the rafters and cast sinister shadows on everything, making what was ugly even more ugly. Screams of the scouting party ahead of us echoed back and warned us not to turn in a particular direction or climb staircases.

"We should find the undercroft where the cellars lay," I whispered to Athelstan when I caught him up.

"What are you doing?!" he snapped. "Go back outside." He said to one of his huscarls, "Ulmar, take the Princess back."

"No!" I said, pulling free. "I will find my parents. It is my pledge. Let me go." Athelstan and Ulmar looked at one another. "Sirs, you waste time. Let me go and I will find my parents."

"Not if you're maimed. Or worse.

Eleanor, you can't be here."

"I'm staying."

Athelstan gave me a wary, unhappy look, and without taking his eyes from me, motioned the fyrd onward. "Ulmar protect the princess. And you, Princess, stay with me."

"I will," I answered and for reassurance took his hand.

We found ourselves in the great hall and knew it was such for the thrones upon the dais at the end of the chamber, and the gigantic statues of Thorne's ancestors set apart like support beams every yard or so. The marble likenesses were also being choked by the bracken. We walked through unmolested. The sounds of chains rattling somewhere in the room made everyone reach for a weapon if they did not already grasp the pommel of a sword or an ax handle, the shaft of a spear. It came from the middle of the hall.

A huscarl stumbled suddenly and fell into what was a gaping hole in the center of the room: an oubliette. His shout as he fell and then the sickening thud as he landed God knew where made us stop. We heard a woman's gasp and then the chink and rattle of metal.

"He's probably dead. God rest his soul," I whispered. Athelstan and several others crossed themselves as I did.

The only sound then was our labored, frightened breathing. We waited, looking about.

"Who's there?"

My father's voice made my heart leap. Before Athelstan could hold me back, I ran to the oubliette and looked down, smiling through my tears.

"Only me, Eleanor," I said.

"My Ella!" Mother exclaimed.

"Is it really you?" Father asked. "Tell me!"

"I swear it, Father! I'm Eleanor, your daughter."

"Only my daughter could know the answer to this question," Father said. "What was the name of my horse when I was the Prince of the Sapphire Hills before I came to Rosemyre to wed your mother?"

"Granite; because he was as gray and speckled as the stone, and he was swift and strong. You rode him too hard through the vale near the Caves at Wormhill in your haste to claim your bride. He threw a shoe and fell and broke his leg. You had to walk the rest of the way to Rosemyre. They called you the Beggar Prince, for your clothes were in tatters, and you wore your boots through. You had to carry your saddlebags."

Father started to weep and I reached down, hoping to take his hand. Alas, they were chained and could only move so far. Still, we tried to reach one another. The lamplight above us illuminated what I suspected. My parents showed signs of torture and were thin and pale. Their clothes were dirty and they were stripped of their jewelry, even their wedding rings. There were ragged patches where the stones had been torn from my mother's skirt and bodice. She had bruising and cuts around her face and her long, lovely neck. *I didn't want to think. . .*

"Is there a ladder or rope?" I asked, looking around. The huscarls started to search and a few were even more resourceful: they had taken off shirts and cloaks and tore or cut them into strips, then tied them together to make a rope. That was attached to my banner pole, which Master Moorehead lowered down and Athelstan and a huscarl shimmied into the prison cell.

"Athelstan of Worthy!" my father cried happily. "You are a most welcome sight."

"We'll share a cup of ale when all this is done. What do you say? For now, we'll relieve you of these chains," and saying this, he used Ulmar's ax to break my parents' bonds, and once free, Mother and Father embraced unencumbered, whispered endearments, and turned to embrace Athelstan and offer thanks.

"Someone comes!" one of the guards cried hoarsely. All activity stopped and we listened.

Footsteps on a stairwell and voices in argument.

"It's Thorne," Ulmar said.

"Quickly now," Athelstan whispered.

My mother and then my father was brought up out of captivity. Our reunion was brief, for the enemy grew near. "Can you walk?" I asked my parents, glancing at their swollen, bare, and bloody feet.

"We'll run if we must," said my father, looking at Mother and taking her hand.

"Then we must go now."

The bracken started to shriek and

writhe as we sped as fast as we were able through the hall and to the courtyard, retracing our steps. Soldiers jumped in our path but the fyrd attacked and fought them off. No sooner was a Thorne man down than another came from around a corner or stairwell. We ducked, dove, and ran as fast as we could, finally making it to the bailey where the rest of the armies waited. Upon seeing my father, the angels bowed as one with the fyrd.

"Hail, King Humphrey! Hail, Queen Alienor!" they cried.

When Athelstan emerged with his guard, the cheers were deafening. "All hail, Athelstan of Worthy, Worthy of The Greenhavens!"

"Why, look at your smile and blushes," Mother teased and gently brushed the hair off my face in the loving manner I'd missed for so many years and now brought tears of joy. "A Worthy husband will it be?" she asked.

I continued to smile and lowered my head, nodding in agreement. "I will have none other. But that will be Athelstan's decision."

My mother nodded in greeting to

Athelstan, who knelt to kiss her extended hand. He then knelt before me and returned the garter. Athelstan kissed the bright blue length of silk after removing it from his leg and then before everyone, gave me a kiss that was more loving than cordial.

"I think he's decided," my mother said, winking at me.

We mounted up, and I, giving my chestnut to Mother, rode pillion with Athelstan. It was a delight to have his arm around me as we led my parents and the armies out of the castle bailey and across the moors to the vale and above where the road led back to Flowergate and further south, to Rosemyre.

I leaned against him, weary both in body and spirit. If the angels could bear us on their wings and take us home, it would be another gift from God. However, as we rode south, the angel army gradually disappeared until there were only the guardian angels and the Archangels in our cohort.

"Tonight we will rest in my father's castle and then we'll ride to Rosemyre," Athelstan whispered as I drifted off to sleep. I didn't sleep long, for the army's sudden halt and the acrid stench of smoke woke me. We were at the gates of Stokeland, the main town in Worthy's principality in The Greenhavens.

Nothing was green here.

"What is it?" I asked sleepily.

"The damn fool," Athelstan swore. "He'll pay—by my saints and angels, he'll pay!"

Thorne and his army had gone ahead of us and sacked the town. He waited for us at the market cross, surrounded by his three sons. Buildings that weren't alight or destroyed were now being encroached upon by the bracken we'd seen at Bramble Court. As people fled, the bracken lashed out and struck anyone close enough to be a victim. I watched the townspeople fall to their deaths on the deadly thorns.

"Your celebration ends here and now!" Thorne shouted at us and pointed at flames licking the dirt. Demons materialized from the soot and ash. "The people want a new life and the promise of such! I am the only man who can give them this. I alone can bring peace! Humphrey Willoughby, you are a relic of the past!"

"Stand ready!" Athelstan shouted to his men, looking to them and the demons.

"Give me a sword!" Father demanded. Mother and I were ready with protests but our army cheered more. One of Athelstan's huscarls handed him his own sword.

"Alienor! For my queen!" Father shouted. "For Rosemyre!" Then he limped forward and led men into a new fray.

Ariella was ready to take us away from the battle but she succeeded in only taking Mother. I climbed on my chestnut steed and galloped into the thick of fighting with Michael and Raphael on either side of me.

The feel of my sword meeting others was like a lightning bolt coursing up my arm. I do not know if I killed anyone, nor did I care. I would avenge the wrongs done to my family and kingdom.

Townspeople now crept from their hiding places carrying weapons and anything that could be used as weapons. The rally cries of "*We Are Worthy!*" and "*Athelstan!*" continued until we were an army a hundred or more strong, shoulder to shoulder, as we fought the demons.

Defenders of the Castle of Worthy now poured from the gatehouse and over the drawbridge, praising God and Worthy.

I was still on my horse, attacking where I could and rallying the fyrd with my father and Athelstan. Whether Raphael and Michael shielded me from death, I do not know, for they were as busy as we mortals in vanquishing the enemy.

"Thorne's been taken! His banner is down!" Ulmar cried, pointing with his sword, and the army rejoiced.

"Ella! Behind you!"

Father's warning was too late. I turned, expecting one of Thorne's men, and saw the demon towering over me with an ax.

I was looking into Hell—that was the only way to describe the dead eyes, the green skin with lesions that wept and glowed with fire, and the mouth with lips stretched back to show the teeth and bones of its mouth in a perpetual grimace. I could see the outline of his skeleton and, even more frightening, a pale, yellow heart barely beating in his chest.

The demon raised his ax and I ducked under his arm to stab straight into his heart. As I was doing this, I heard the scream and saw Athelstan fall. The demon laughed and raised his ax again but it shattered into dust as if a wall of glass protected me.

The Archangels now encircled me and they attacked the rest of the demons, who fell, one by one, until there were none.

Thorne and his sons knelt at the market cross, my father's prisoners. Father waved with his sword at one of the huscarls to take them away. I heard later that angels flew down that night and took off with them to who knew where, but I could guess.

The day was ours. All around me people were laughing and weeping tears of joy, embracing one other as the bracken that for a moment held the town its prisoner fell away to dust, revealing the brightly-colored exteriors of surviving houses and shops and the pure, glistening white of the towers and keep.

Midst the chanting and laughter meant for my father and Athelstan, I heard nothing, for my prince, my beloved Athelstan, lay still on the cobblestones, his armor pierced near his heart and smeared with blood and gore.

Raphael and I knelt at Athelstan's side.

"Athelstan, come back to me!" I sobbed. "My prince and friend!"

I kissed his lips and found them still warm, but there was no response from him. No gleam or sparkle from his eyes. Once again, I kissed him and would have given way to grief when again there was no response when Raphael unfurled his wings and enclosed us in the protection of the shimmering multi-colored feathers that sparkled silver.

The light was like the sunlight at noon on the waters of the bay at Flowergate. It was bright, almost painful, and I couldn't look away. Finally, Raphael moved back and stood. It was then Athelstan opened his eyes and smiled. "Hello, Princess," he said weakly.

Raphael carried him into the castle where he rested for three days, and then, on Christmas morning, we rode from Worthy to Flowergate, where we met grateful subjects who joined our cavalcade and escorted us to Rosemyre.

Church bells rang for hours on the day several weeks later when I was married to

Athelstan in the cathedral, Olivia and Oliver carrying my train, my parents watching tearfully proud as I consented to be a wife, good and true, to a Worthy prince. Were they tears of joy that their daughter had found love and would be Queen of Rosemyre in her time, or that their daughter finally behaved as a princess should?

After all, it was a lot to expect from The Shop Girl of Flowergate.

WRV

ACKNOWLEDGMENTS

MY THANKS to Hans Christian Andersen, the Brothers, Grimm, and Andrew Lang for their stories, which kept me up well past my bedtime and still captivate my imagination today.

It's never too late to read a fairy tale.

Or write one to share.

ABOUT THE AUTHOR

ELLEN L. EKSTROM is a native of the San Francisco Bay Area and was educated locally. She holds a bachelor's degree in theological studies. Her area of concentration is Christian Mythos, also known as church history, with a sub-specialty in Christian Social Ethics, for both of which she took honors. Ellen has been fascinated by all things medieval since childhood and is now studying Late Anglo-Saxon England to prepare two forthcoming novels, *Swannsaeld* and *The Sometime Queen*.

The genres Ellen prefers to work in are fantasy/historical: her first novel was *The Legacy*, a tale of fourteenth-century Florence and Tuscany, followed by her retelling of the St. George and the Dragon legend, *Armor of Light*, and its sequel, the stand-alone novel *Ascalon*, and *St. Edmund Wood*, a story of Victorian England. Occasionally, she delves into matters of the modern heart, as evidenced by her novels in the *Midwinter Sonata* series and *What She Wished For... a Cautionary Tale*. Just as a painter has many subjects to bring to a canvas, Ellen believes that there are many stories to tell, and to limit oneself to a niche isn't the way she lives and thinks.

Want to know more about Whyte Rose & Violet, Scribes? Go to **www.whyteroseandviolet.net/about**.